KUNG FU DRAGON POLE

by William Cheung

Editor: Mike Lee
Graphic Design: Karen Massad
Art Production: Sergio Onaga
Cover Design: Sergio Onaga

Printed in the United States of America
Library of Congress Catalog Card Number: 86-42769
ISBN 0-89750-107-1

Fourth printing 1998

WARNING

This book is presented only as a means of preserving a unique aspect of the heritage of the martial arts. Neither Ohara Publications nor the author makes any representation, warranty or guarantee that the techniques described or illustrated in this book will be safe or effective in any self-defense situation or otherwise. You may be injured if you apply or train in the techniques illustrated in this book. To minimize the risk of training injury, nothing described or illustrated in this book should be undertaken without personal, expert instruction. In addition, it is essential that you consult a physician regarding whether or not to attempt anything described in this book. Federal, state or local law may prohibit the use or possession of any of the weapons described or illustrated in this book. Specific self-defense responses illustrated in this book may not be justified in any particular situation in view of all of the circumstances or under the applicable federal, state or local law. Neither Ohara Publications nor the author makes any representation or warranty regarding the legality or appropriateness of any weapon or technique mentioned in this book.

OHARA PUBLICATIONS, INCORPORATED
SANTA CLARITA, CALIFORNIA

Dedication

This book is dedicated to my teacher, the late Yip Man, to the world-wide martial arts community as a whole, and to the followers of wing chun in particular.

Acknowledgement

I would like to thank my friend, Dan Inosanto, the great escrima and jeet kune do expert, and the very talented martial artist Ken Teichmann, for helping to demonstrate the techniques in this book. I would also like to thank Lloyd Macey for writing the foreword.

About the Author

At the age of ten, William Cheung started his training in wing chun kung fu under Yip Man. When he was 14 he decided to follow wing chun as a way of life. He trained full-time under Yip Man's roof, and for the next four years, wing chun took up all of his time. Between 1957 and 1958 Cheung won the Kung Fu Elimination Contests in Hong Kong, defeating opponents with many more years of experience. During that period, he helped to teach Bruce Lee many of the techniques that he would later use in his very successful film career.

After Cheung left Hong Kong in 1959 to pursue his academic studies in Australia, he continued his training in wing chun kung fu. It was not until 1974 that he started teaching professionally in Melbourne. That year also saw the foundation of the Australian Kung Fu Federation and Cheung's appointment as chairman.

In 1978-79 Cheung was the chief instructor for the U.S. Navy Seventh Fleet for unarmed combat at the U.S. base in Yukosuka, Japan.

Cheung has appeared on such Australian television shows as *The Daryl Somers Show, The Don Lane Show, The Mike Walsh Show* and various news and radio interviews. He has also made television appearances in Hong Kong, Japan, New Zealand, and America.

He is frequently featured in newspapers and magazine articles and has appeared on the cover of martial arts magazines BLACK BELT and KARATE/KUNG FU ILLUSTRATED. Previously he has authored *Kung Fu Butterfly Swords* for Ohara. In 1983 he was named to the BLACK BELT magazine Hall of Fame.

Foreword

William Cheung is one of the world's foremost exponents and authorities on wing chun kung fu and the weaponry associated with the style.

Over many years, initially in Hong Kong, then Australia, and now throughout the world, William Cheung has proven his expertise and ability in the art which at a very young age, he chose as a way of life. Today, his knowledge is eagerly sought around the world. He travels to the United States twice a year to conduct seminars on wing chun and its weaponry.

In this book, Cheung explores the techniques of the wing chun dragon pole. This art practiced correctly is truly an extension of nature. As in nature, the use of force against force only results in lost energy with a potentially disasterous outcome. If a tree does not bend with the wind, it breaks. So it is with the dragon pole techniques. It is essential to economize energy and conserve strength, and so, force against force is never employed. The basic principle behind the art is to bend with the force and spring back to counter the attack, just as the bough of the tree returns to its former position when the gust subsides.

It is also essential for the continuation and improvement of the art that wing chun dragon pole techniques continue to be passed on from teacher to student. With his wealth of experience and knowledge, no one is more qualified than William Cheung to present the techniques of the wing chun dragon pole.

—Lloyd Macey

Introduction

This book is written as a reference for the keen martial artist to reveal to him the ancient wing chun secrets of fighting with the dragon pole. Wing chun is a scientific approach to fighting, especially in weapons where one cannot afford to make the slightest mistake, and where every move and counter move has its specific purpose.

In addition to the dragon pole techniques, a comprehensive history and background on the dragon pole are included. Further, this book describes the wing chun warm up exercises and training drills for the dragon pole. Hence, it is sincerely hoped that this unique manual for weapon practitioners is a beneficial contribution to martial arts.

Presently, William Cheung's World Wing Chun Association headquarters are located at: Second Floor, 26A Corrs Lane, Melbourne 3000, Australia and 5040 West Jean Avenue, Las Vegas, Nevada. Telephone (03) 663-4613 in Australia and (702) 646-5097 in the United States.

Origins of the Dragon Pole

As far back as 3000 B.C., the staff and long pole were used in hunting as well as in battle. The staff is a stick between five and six feet in length, both ends of the same diameter. The long pole can be as long as 13 feet, and one end tapered. These weapons were easy to construct and were very popular in ancient days.

With the discovery of bronze and iron, the staff and long pole were modified into weapons such as spears, big choppers, and various versions of the long stick with metal casting at the end.

Use of the staff and long pole was also popular among the Shaolin monks during the early Sung Dynasty (A.D. 960-1279). During that time the monks were involved in helping the first emperor, Sung, establish his kingdom. The staff and long pole were used extensively by the monks, who, because of their religion, did not like sharp edged weapons that would inflict undue injury to their enemies.

Even after the Sung Dynasty, the Shaolin monks continued to favor the use of the staff and long pole. In the Ching Dynasty (1644-1911) the monks used these weapons to defend themselves from the Ching government's siege on the Shaolin Temple.

There were many forms of staff and long pole in the shaolin style, but the most effective was the Six-and-a-Half-Strike Dragon Pole, originated by Grandmaster Gee Sin.

According to Chinese legend, Grandmaster Gee Sin was also one of the five grandmasters who developed the wing chun style. But Yim Wing Chun, who became the only heir to the wing chun style, and after whom it was named, did not learn the dragon pole as part of her wing chun training. She left the Shaolin Temple having learned only the empty-hand techniques and the butterfly swords which she passed on to her husband Leung Bok Cho.

The dragon pole descended from Grandmaster Gee Sin through three generations of his family to Wong Wah Bo, and was reunited with the wing chun style by another twist of fate.

Yim Wing Chun's husband, Leung Bok Cho, in searching for someone to whom he could pass on the wing chun system chose one of his nephews. Coincidentally, this also turned out to be Wong Wah Bo, the third generation heir to the dragon pole techniques of Grandmaster Gee Sin.

Wong Wah Bo was a very popular opera star on a floating opera barge called *The Red Boat*. One day, Leung Bok Cho went to *The Red Boat* to see the opera. Leung and Wong got together after the show, and came to the agreement that they would have a friendly martial art contest. If Leung could defeat Wong easily, then Wong would undertake to learn the wing chun system.

The two confronted each other on the stage of *The Red Boat*. Wong was armed with a 12-foot dragon pole and Leung had a pair of butterfly swords each measuring 18 inches. Since Wong considered himself as having the advantage, he asked Leung to attack first. Leung brandished the pair of butterfly swords to begin his attack. Wong was very cautious in defending because the swords were sharp and Leung's technique was very tight and swift. Though he fought with all his might, Wong found it very difficult to fend off Leung's attack. He was forced to retreat to the edge of the stage. Now, Wong could not but use the most deadly technique of the Six-and-a-Half-Strike Dragon Pole to deal with the situation. When Leung aimed a double slash with both swords at Wong's head, Wong raised his pole in a technique called *bon kwun* to neutralize the assault, and followed up with a lower jab to Leung's leg. This was one of the most efficient dragon pole techniques in the Six-and-a-Half-Strike Dragon Pole because block and counterattack were almost simultaneous. Wong used it swiftly and thought this would surely bring a speedy victory. Nevertheless, quite unexpectedly, Wong felt something cold touch his hand. He looked down and found the sharp edge of a butterfly sword resting on his wrist. He had no alternative. He dropped the dragon pole and admitted defeat. Wong fell to his knees and begged to be Leung's student so that he could learn the wing chun system.

From that brief encounter Leung realized that he had chosen well and that Wong had the potential of becoming the best. After Wong mastered wing chun, he improved the Six-and-a-Half-Strike Dragon Pole by combining it with wing chun and making its techniques much more effective.

Contents

CHAPTER 1

Exercises for the Dragon Pole

It is essential that the practitioner use the dragon pole as an extension of his arms. Agility also plays a major role in acquiring proficiency with the weapon. This chapter therefore includes exercises for strengthening the legs and the torso, and for training coordination and mobility with the dragon pole.

Conditioning

Basic Strengthening and Coordination Exercise

(1) From the ready position with feet together, (2&3) extend your arms out at shoulder level with your hands open and palms down. (4) Close your hands into fists. Turn your fists palms up, and (5) pull your fists back at chest level alongside your body. (6) Flex your knees, and (7) step out to the right with your right foot into a horse stance. (8) Turn and punch to the right with your left fist. (9) Face

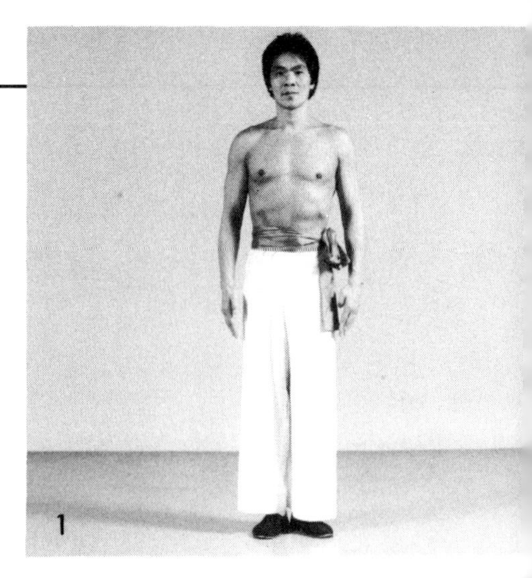
1

4

7

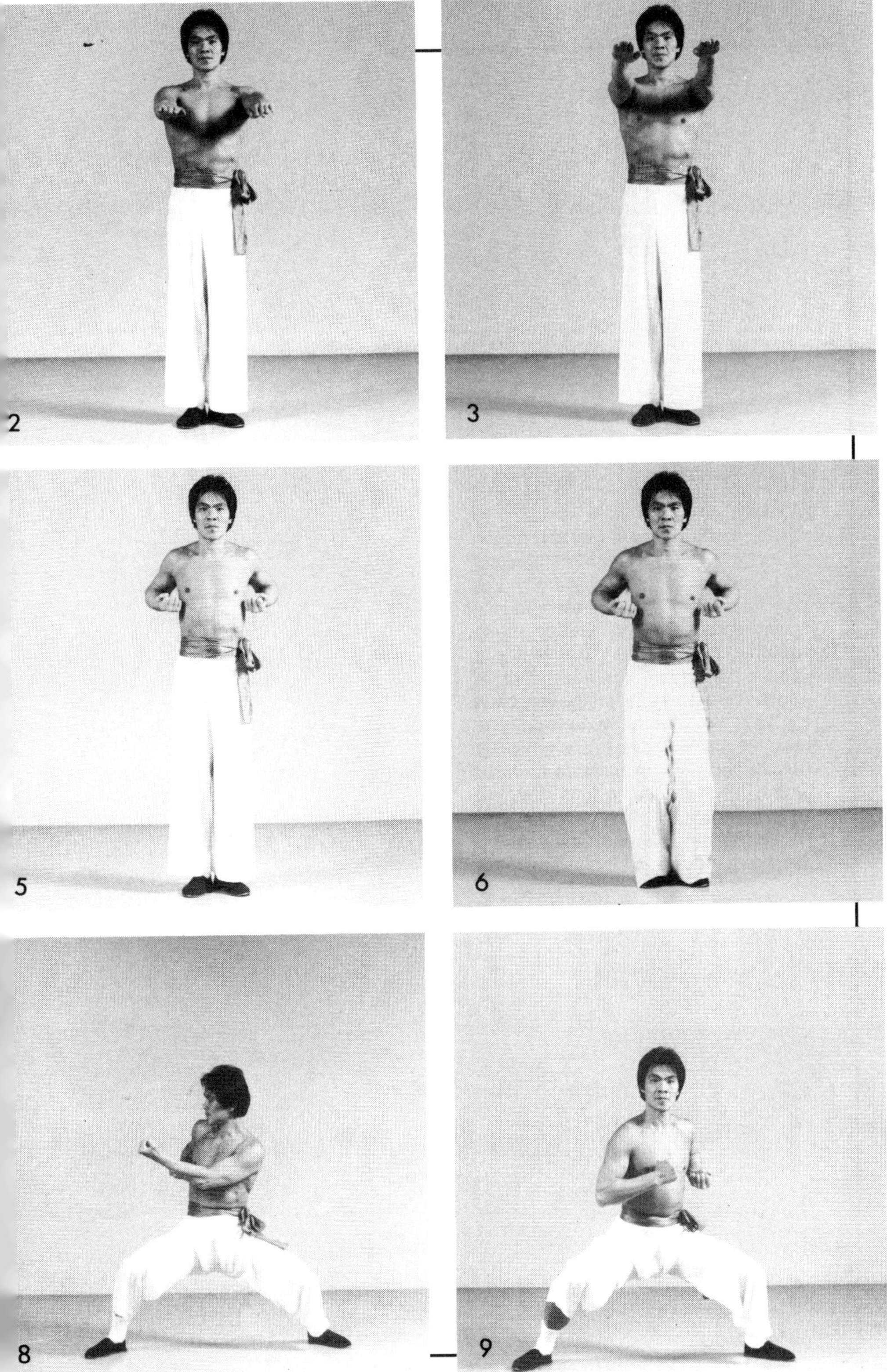

 Continued

forward. (10&11) Take a half step to the left with your left foot and punch to the left with your right fist, pulling your left fist back to your body. (12) Withdraw your right fist back toward your body as you (13&14) take another half step to the left and punch to the left with your left fist, (15) pulling your right all the way back to your body at full extension. (16) Repeat the half step to the left once again and (17&18) punch with your right fist at the same time that you retract your left fist next to your body. Repeat this exercise stepping to the right.

 Continued

Footwork Training Without the Dragon Pole

1

Footwork Training Without the Dragon Pole

In this exercise you will learn footwork and hand movements as well as the names of the major techniques which you will run into in more detail later. (1) Establish a front stance with 60 percent of your weight on your back leg and 40 percent on the front, the heel of the front foot lifted. (2) Take a half side step to left with your right foot, distributing your weight evenly on both legs. (3) Take a half side step to the right with your right foot, distributing 60 percent of your weight on your back leg and 40 percent on your front. (4&5) Bring your left foot towards your right foot. (6) Step across to the left with your left foot. (7) Execute an imaginary block in which you raise your arms as if slanting the pole from a high to a low position to execute a block. This is the bon kwun position. (8) Step with

3

6

5

Continued

your right foot out to the right into a horse stance and execute an imaginary thrust to the right. Thrusting is called bil kwun. (9) Withdraw your right foot and come back to the ready position. This is called kwun jong. (10) Withdraw your right foot and position your arms in the bon kwun position as before. (11) Step back with your left foot. As you step back, perform an imaginary block in which you quickly flip the tip of the pole counterclockwise through three quarters of a circle from low to high and back down to the middle level. This is called fok kwun. (12) Withdraw your right foot and come back to kwun jong ready position. (13) Step across with your right foot and execute an imaginary block in which you swing the tip of the pole through a counterclockwise arc from high to low. This is called garn kwun. (14) Step across with your left foot and execute an imaginary upward bil kwun. (15) Turn across to the right with the imaginary pole at chest level as if preparing to execute a downward hitting block. Here you are simply preparing to push both hands straight down simultaneously. Such a striking action would be called tarn kwun.

8

10

13

1
12

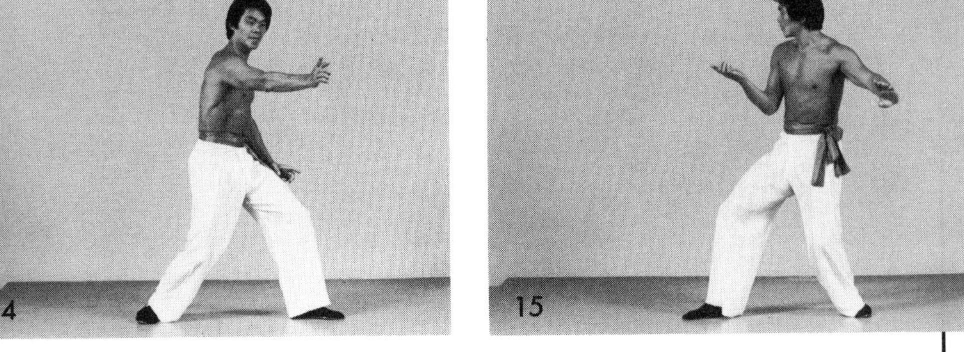
4
15

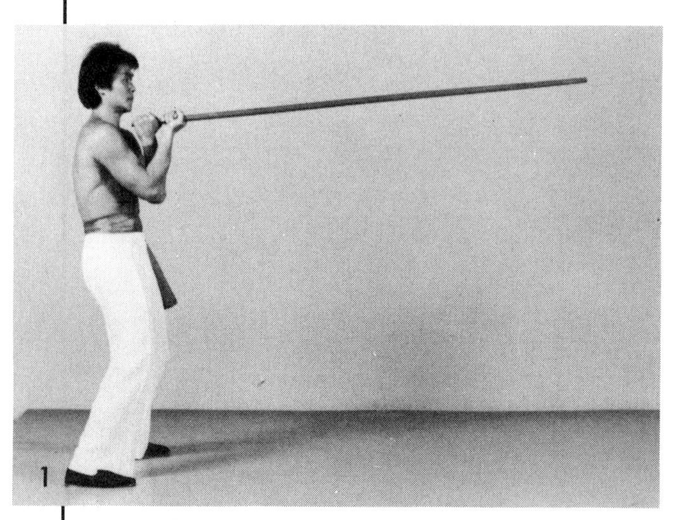

1

Long Arm Strength

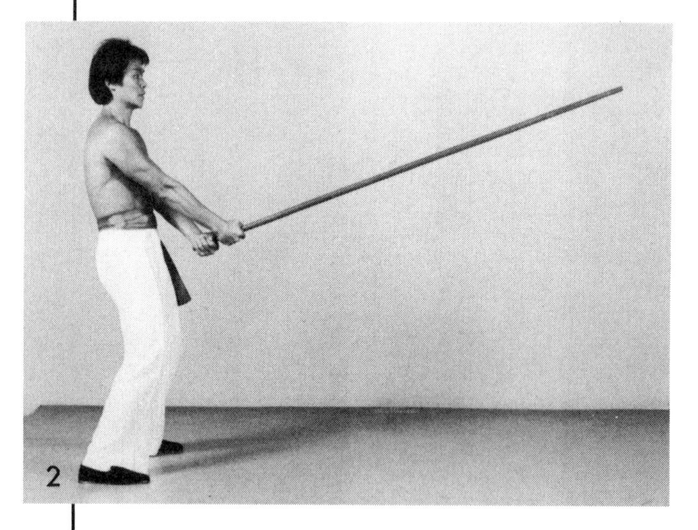

2

Long Arm Strength

(1) Hold the dragon pole at the end with both hands, wrists facing upward, feet apart, knees flexed. (2) Push down sharply, keeping the elbows straight and the tip of the pole steady. (3) Thrust the tip of

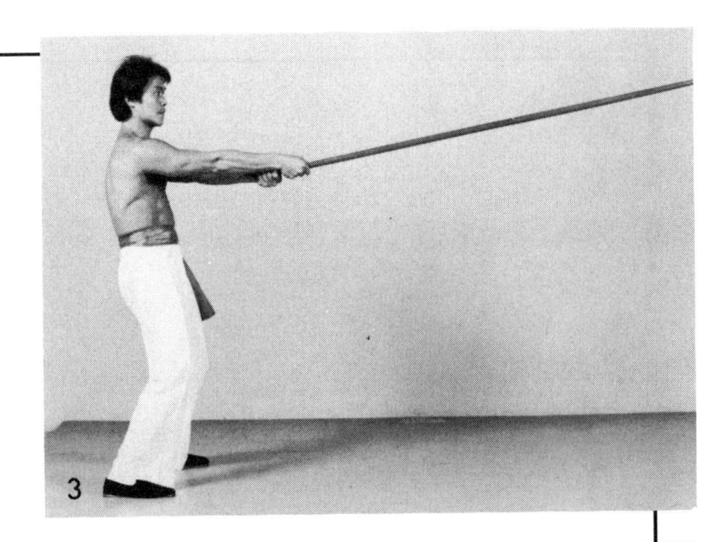

the pole straight ahead, keeping your elbows straight. (4) Push down sharply keeping the elbows straight. (5) Come back to the starting position.

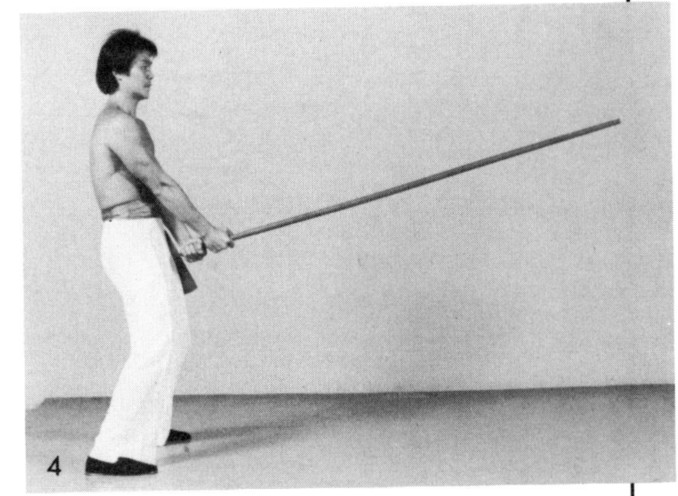

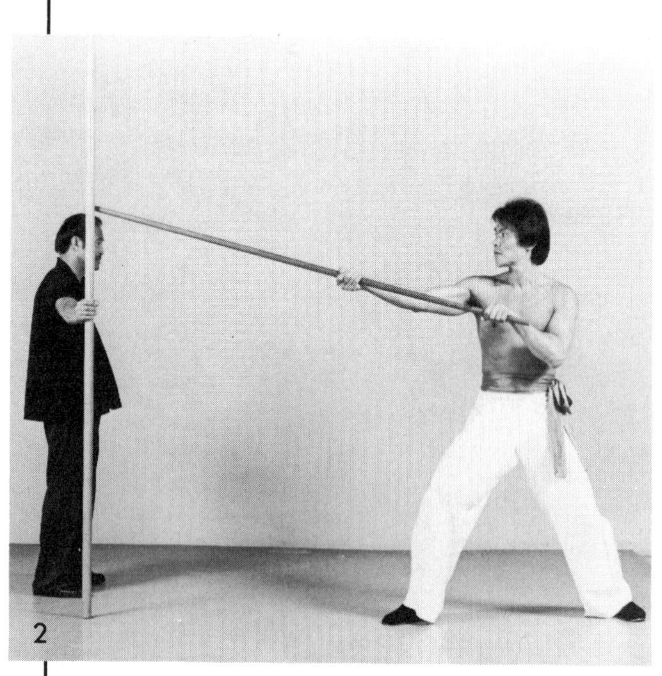

Accuracy Training

Strike from the Side

(1) With your partner holding a pole vertically, begin from the ready position and (2) strike at head level from the side. This is more of a swinging strike than a thrust. The tip of the pole is snapped across horizontally in a forehand motion to contact the target from the side.

Side Thrust

(1) From the ready position with your partner holding the target pole vertically, (2) execute a side thrust. As you bring the pole up from waist level, keep your eye on the target, and as you thrust, you can spy down along the length of the pole to align the pole with the target. It is possible to become extremely accurate with this kind of thrust.

1

2

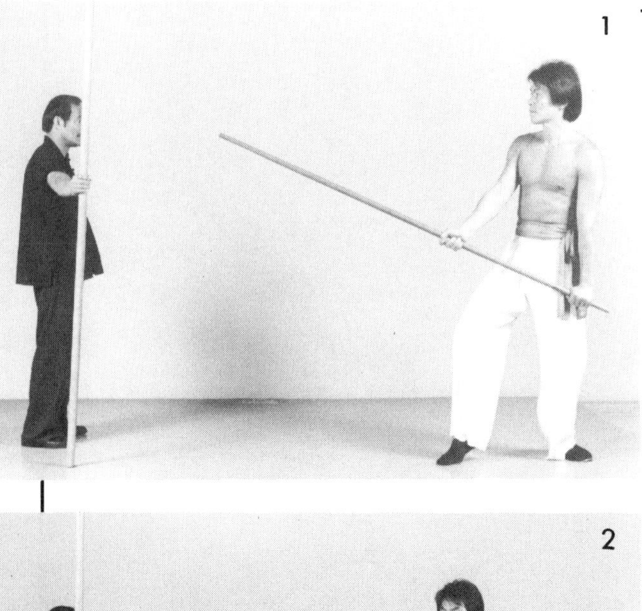

Side Step and Side Thrust

In this exercise a side step is combined with the side thrust technique. (1) From the ready position with your partner holding the target pole in a vertical position, (2) step to the side with your right foot, and spot your target by turning your head. (3) Execute the side thrust at head level. Here the front of your body is turned slightly away from the target, and so the thrust is angled over your right shoulder to some extent.

Step Forward and Low Thrust

(1) From the ready position with your partner holding the target pole in a vertical position, (2) step forward with your right foot into a low horse stance, bringing the dragon pole up to shoulder height. Spot your target, and (3) execute a straight thrust to the midsection.

CHAPTER 2

Basics of Dragon Pole Technique

The length of the dragon pole can vary from six to 13 feet, depending on the availability of the pole and the purpose of the exercise and situation. For instance, practitioners generally train with a heavier, longer pole so that they will be able to build up strength as well as co-ordination at the same time. In an actual combat situation, techniques can be applied to a pole of any length, provided it is no shorter than four feet.

A

B

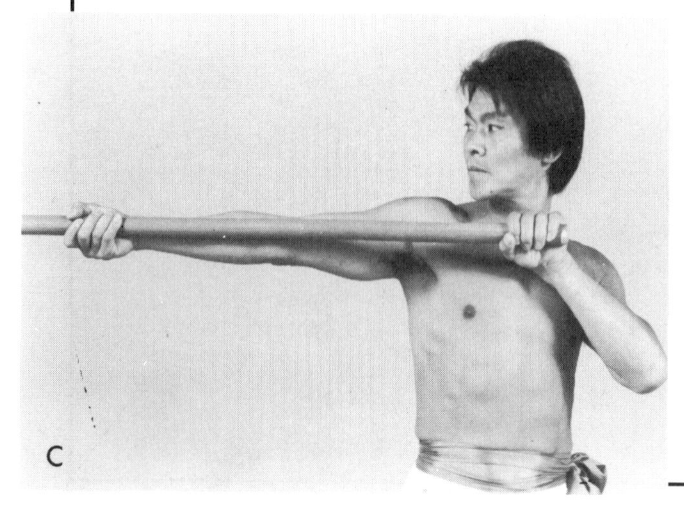

C

Gripping

Correct Way of Holding the Dragon Pole

There are two ways of holding the dragon pole: right handed and left handed. With the right handed dragon pole, the right hand faces inward and the left hand faces outward. These are called the yang and yin hands respectively. The right handed dragon pole is usually held in three common positions: (A) in a low position, (B) at shoulder level, and (C) in a sideward striking position. Note that the left hand should be supporting the end of the pole so that it does not collide with the body or the jaw when force is applied at the other end of the pole.

Blocking

Jut Kwun
(Sharp Downward Block)

(1) From a starting position with the tip pointing at the opponent's head level, (2) snap the pole sharply downward to execute the block. (3) Then lift it back quickly to the starting ready position once again.

1

2

3

Garn Kwun (Diagonal Block— Circular Inward)

(1) Starting with the tip of the dragon pole pointing at the opponent's head level, (2&3) swing the dragon pole so that the tip goes from the head level downward through a counterclockwise arc to a lower position, executing the block.

Fok Kwun (Circular Downward Block)

(1) Starting with the tip of the dragon pole pointing at the opponent's ankle, (2&3) swing the pole so that the tip comes upward through a counterclockwise arc, past the apex of the circle and back down again, describing three-fourths of a complete circle. The intent is to block by coming over the top of the opponent's weapon and knocking it down. Generally this technique is applied to the mid and high section attacks.

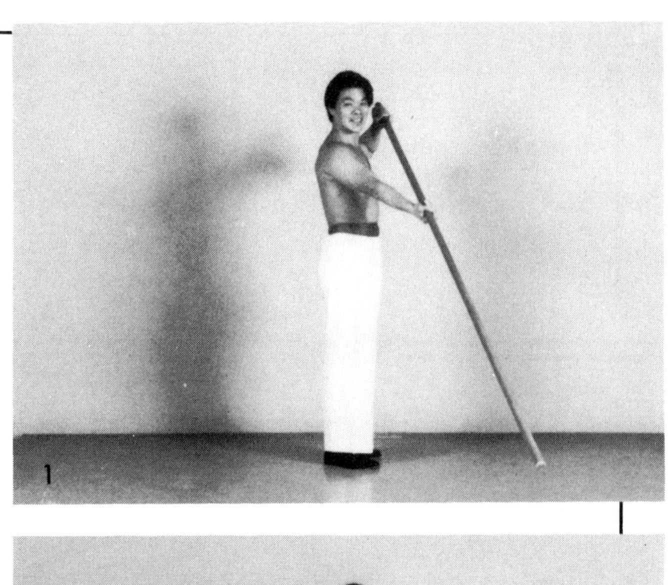

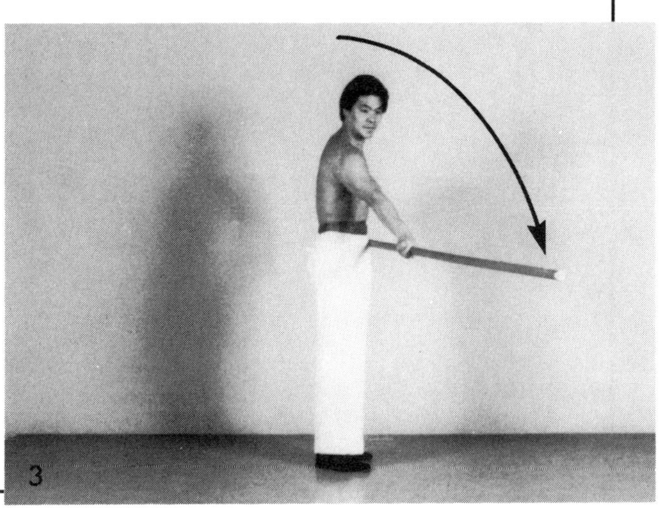

Tan Kwun (Circular Deflection Block From Underneath Upward)

(1) Starting with the tip of the dragon pole pointing to the opponent's head level, (2) swing the pole downward so the tip goes through a counterclockwise arc, past the lowest point of the circle and (3) back up again to (4&5) complete a full circle. The

block is executed by first dropping your pole under your opponent's through the first half of the counterclockwise circle, and then blocking upwards from underneath through the second half of the counterclockwise circle.

 Continued

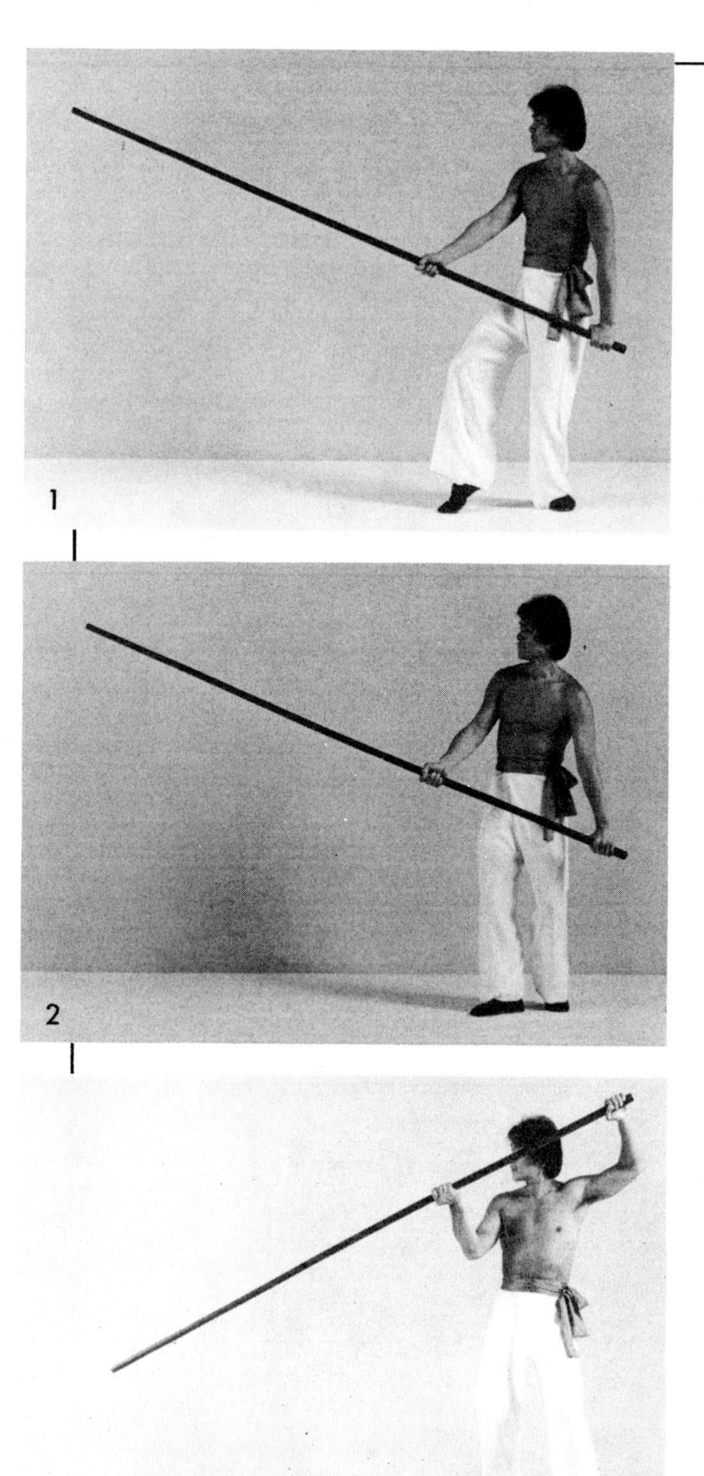

Bon Kwun (Downward Slanting Block)

(1) From a starting position with the tip pointing at the opponent's head level, (2) quickly slant the pole by dropping the tip and (3) raising the end above head level. This block is effective in covering all three levels at once: high, middle and low.

Striking

Tarn Kwun—Forward (Forward Push)

(1) With the dragon pole in a low position, (2) bring it up to shoulder level. (3) Execute a sharp forward push with both arms. Maintain the pole in a horizontal attitude. (4) Pull back quickly following the push to bring the pole back to the ready position.

1

2

3

Tarn Kwun— Downward (Downward Push)

(1) Starting with the dragon pole at shoulder level, maintain the pole in a horizontal attitude, and (2&3) execute a sharp downward push with both arms.

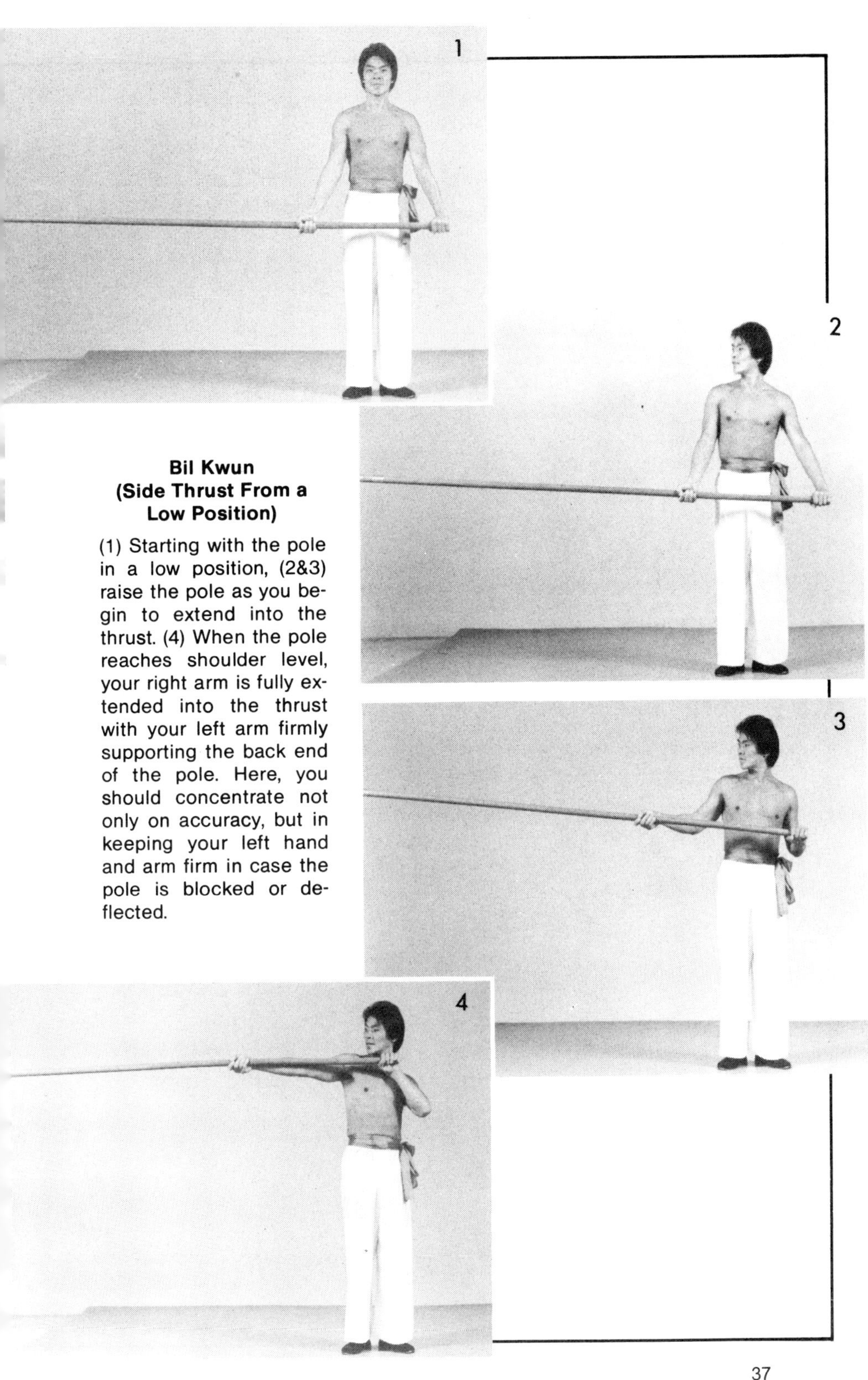

Bil Kwun
(Side Thrust From a Low Position)

(1) Starting with the pole in a low position, (2&3) raise the pole as you begin to extend into the thrust. (4) When the pole reaches shoulder level, your right arm is fully extended into the thrust with your left arm firmly supporting the back end of the pole. Here, you should concentrate not only on accuracy, but in keeping your left hand and arm firm in case the pole is blocked or deflected.

1

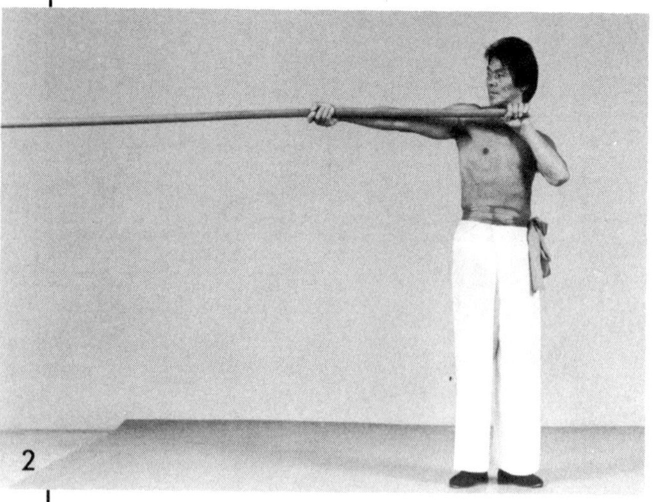
2

Bil Kwun (Side Thrust From Shoulder Level)

(1) With the pole already at shoulder level, bil kwun is executed by (2) thrusting with your right arm out to the right side. It is important always to remind yourself in techniques like this that your left arm and hand must support the back end of the pole firmly. If your support is not strong, a sharp block or deflection at the tip of the pole can cause the end to come back toward your face or neck.

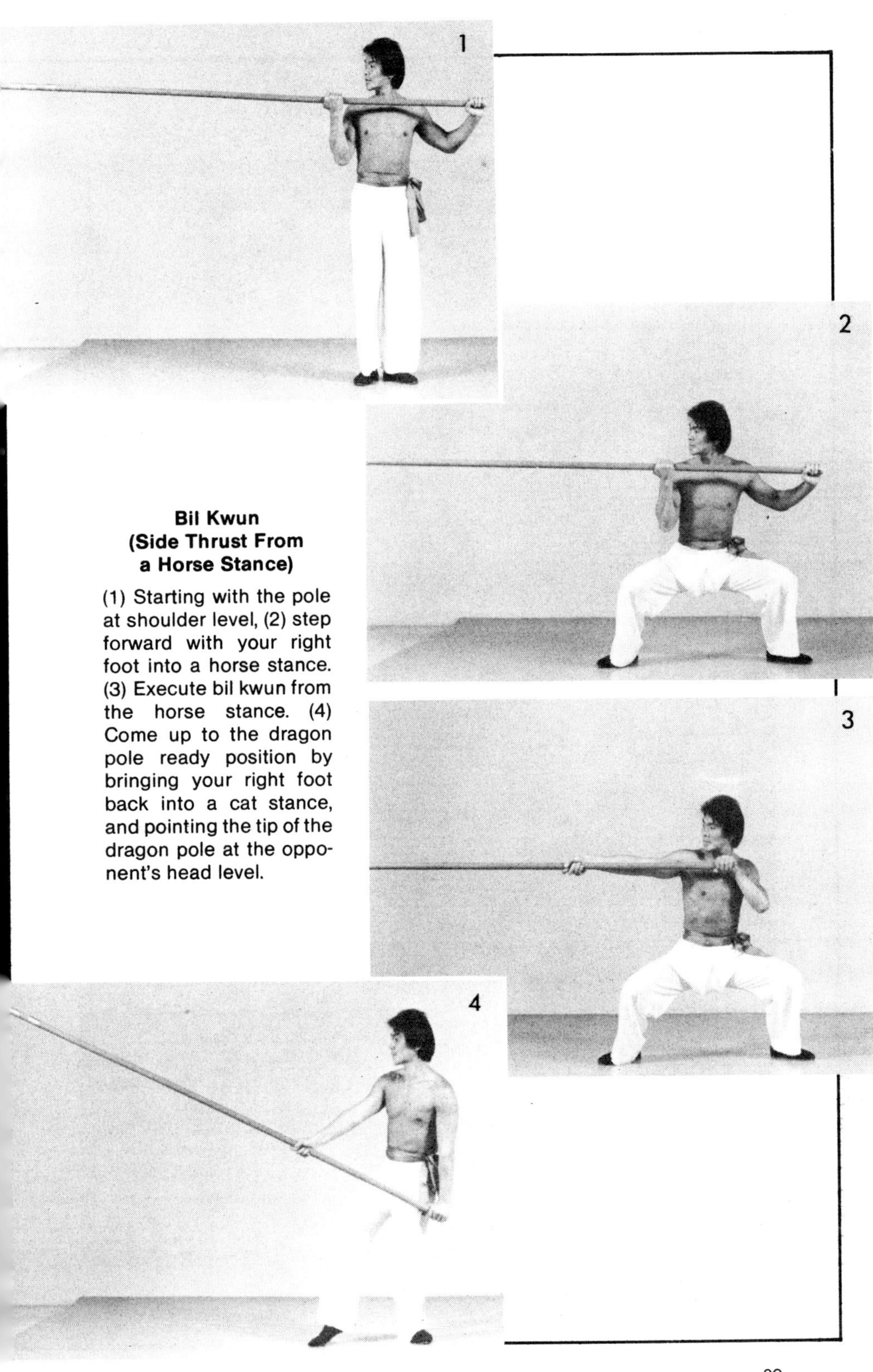

Bil Kwun
(Side Thrust From a Horse Stance)

(1) Starting with the pole at shoulder level, (2) step forward with your right foot into a horse stance. (3) Execute bil kwun from the horse stance. (4) Come up to the dragon pole ready position by bringing your right foot back into a cat stance, and pointing the tip of the dragon pole at the opponent's head level.

CHAPTER 3

Target Areas of the Body

The dragon pole can generate tremendous striking power when used correctly. This makes the dragon pole extremely damaging. Nevertheless, it is important to know that in weapon fighting, the cardinal rule is to attack the secondary targets first, such as the wrists, elbows, knees, insteps or ankles, and then move on to the primary targets such as the solar plexus, throat, temple, side of the head, forehead, and groin.

Target Areas

Elbow

Instep or Ankle

Throat

Solar Plexus

Wrist

Knee

Side of Head

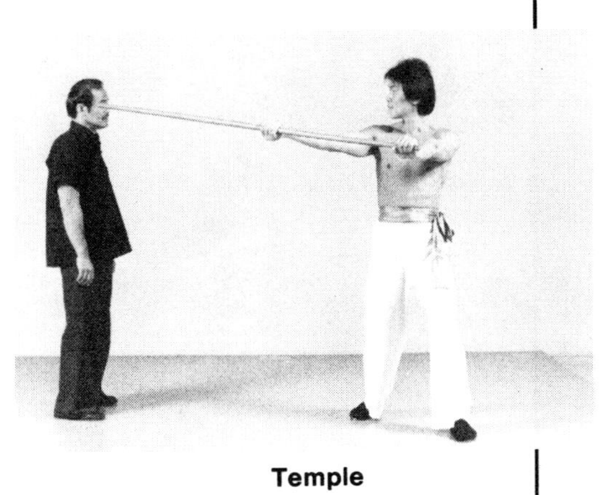

Temple

Forehead

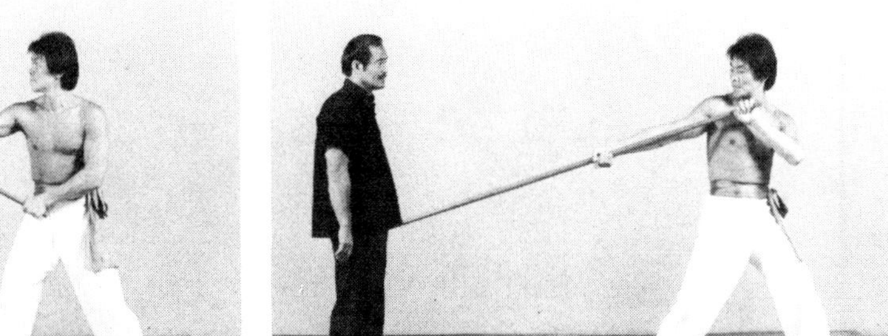

Groin

CHAPTER 4

Louk Dim Book Kwun (Six-and-a-Half-Strike Form)

This form was developed for the wing chun practitioners training in dragon pole techniques to develop strength, speed, coordination, balance, reflexes, mobility, timing, and accuracy. The precision of each movement is of the utmost importance.

Dragon pole striking techniques can be summarized as follows: Front Thrust, Side Thrust, Hit, Semi-Circular Hit, Push with Side of Pole. The defense techniques involve: Tarn Kwun, Garn Kwun, Jut Kwun, Fok Kwun, Tan Kwun, and Huen Kwun. The stances used are: Kwun Jong Stance and Kwun Ma Stance. Side Steps, Forward Steps, and Backward constitute the footwork.

These dragon pole techniques are simple and easy to learn, but the practitioner must take the care to learn them precisely. Weapon fighting does not forgive many mistakes.

Six-and-a-Half-Strike Form

(1) With the pole upright at your left side, (2) raise the pole with your left hand, and grip the pole with your right hand about three feet from the end. (3) Release your left hand grip and bring the pole across your body and place your left hand at the end of the pole. (4) Hold the pole in a horizontal position with arms straight down. (5) Raise the pole still in a horizontal attitude up to shoulder level. (6) Move your right foot out as you execute tarn kwun and point the tip of the pole to head level. (7) Bring the pole to a horizontal attitude at shoulder level, and (8) step toward your imaginary opponent into the kwun ma stance. (9) Thrust horizontally. (10) Bring your

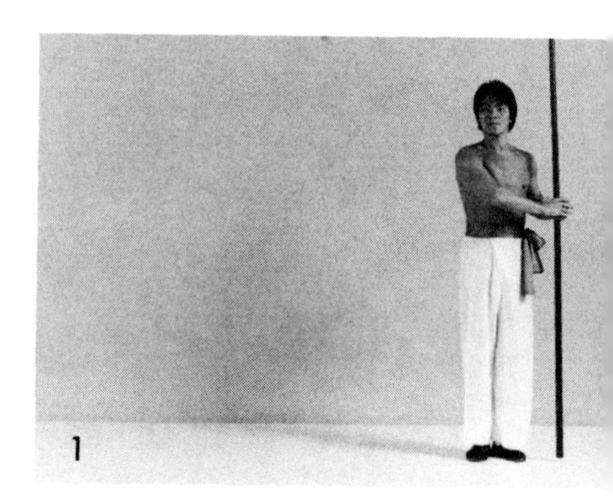
1

4

7

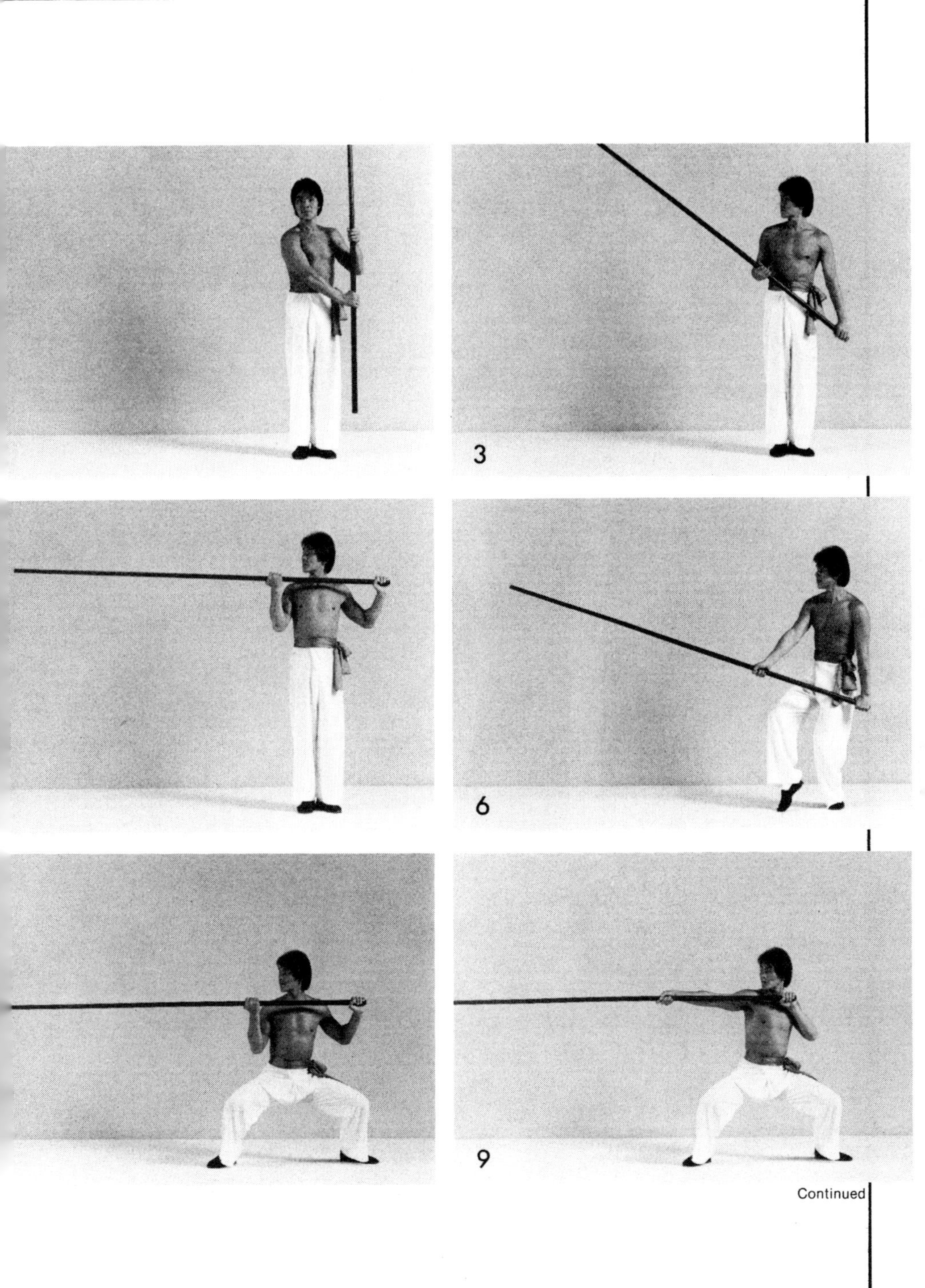

Continued

right foot back as you execute tarn kwun. (11&12) Step across with your left foot, simultaneously raising the pole to shoulder level. (13) Shift your weight to your back foot, and simultaneously strike diagonally downward. (14) Bring the pole back and over, and (15) execute jut kwun. (16) Step to the left and simultaneously execute bon kwun. (17&18) Pull back the pole, and (19&20) execute an

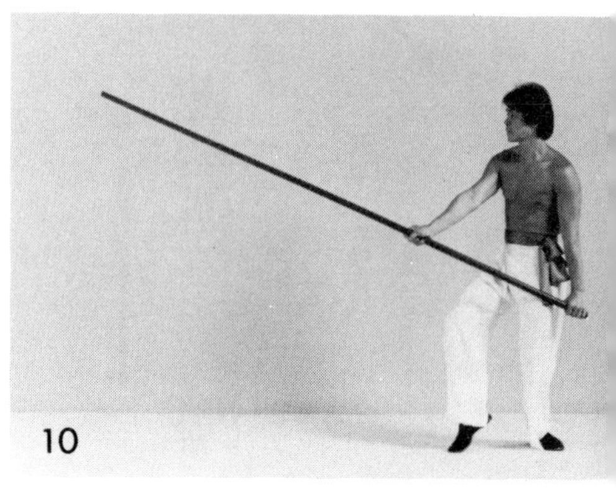
10

13

16

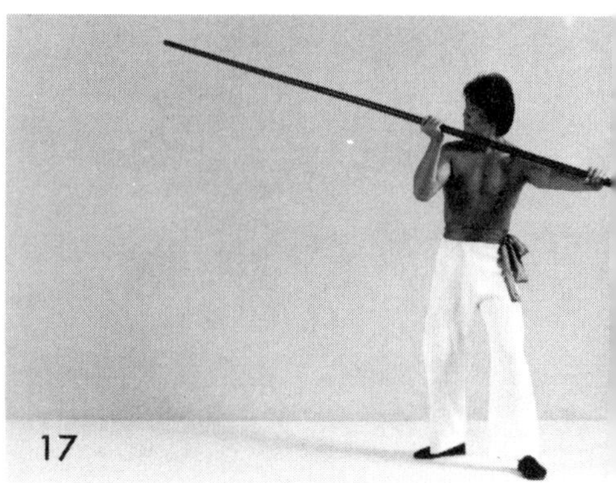
17

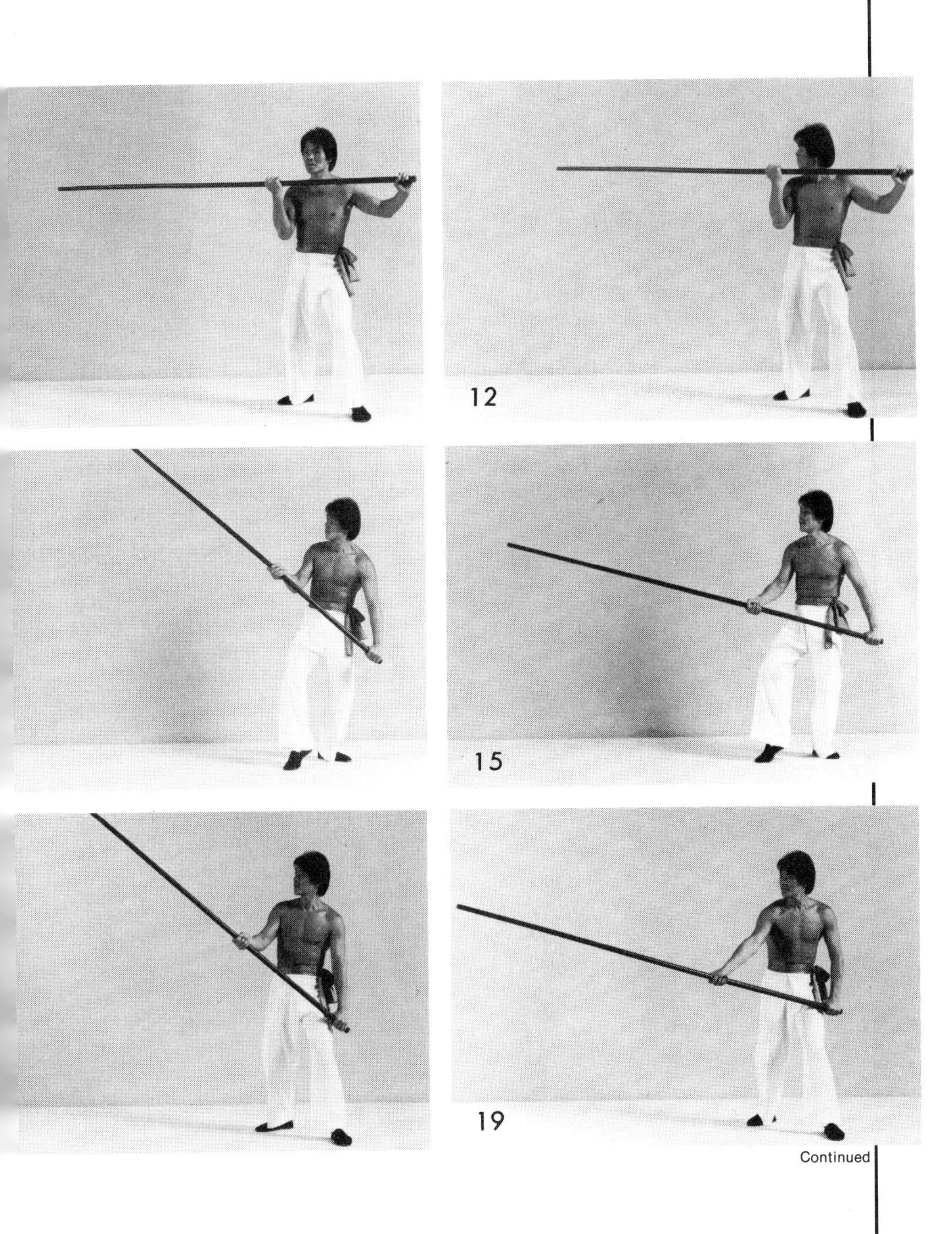

Continued

overhead fok kwun. (21) Raise the tip of the pole, then (22) execute jut kwun and simultaneously thrust forward. (23) Raise the tip of the pole once again. (24) Raise the back end of the pole. (25) Shift your weight to your left foot. (26) Execute fok kwun. (27&28) Step across with your left foot and pull the pole to the extreme left. (29) Execute bon kwun. (30) Step

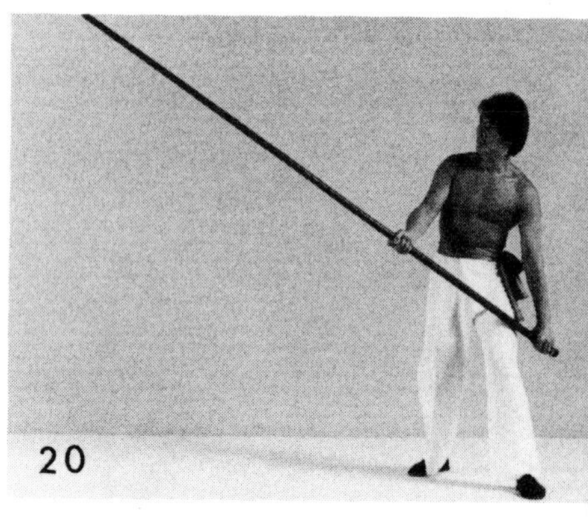
20

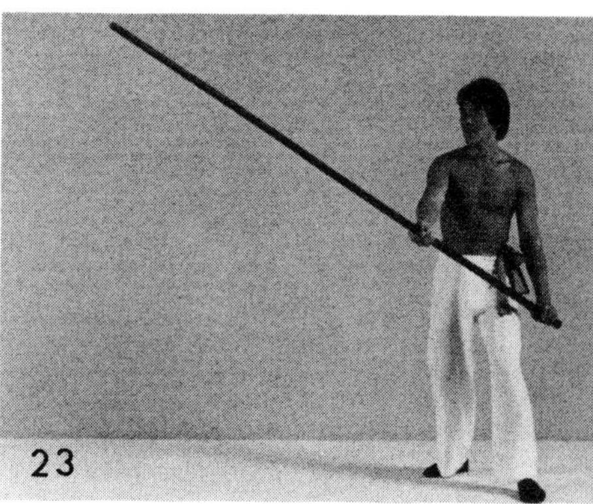
23

26

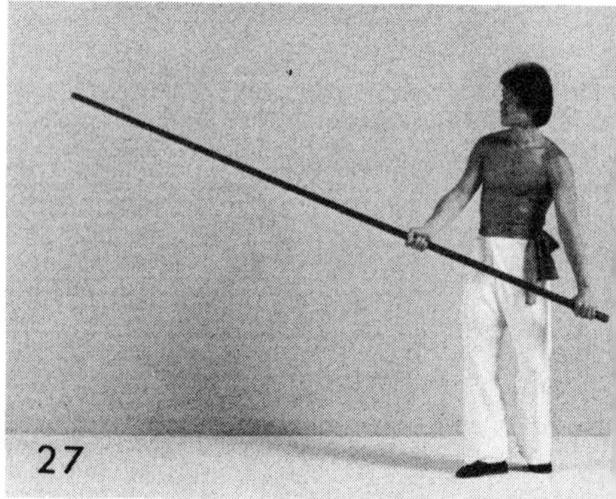
27

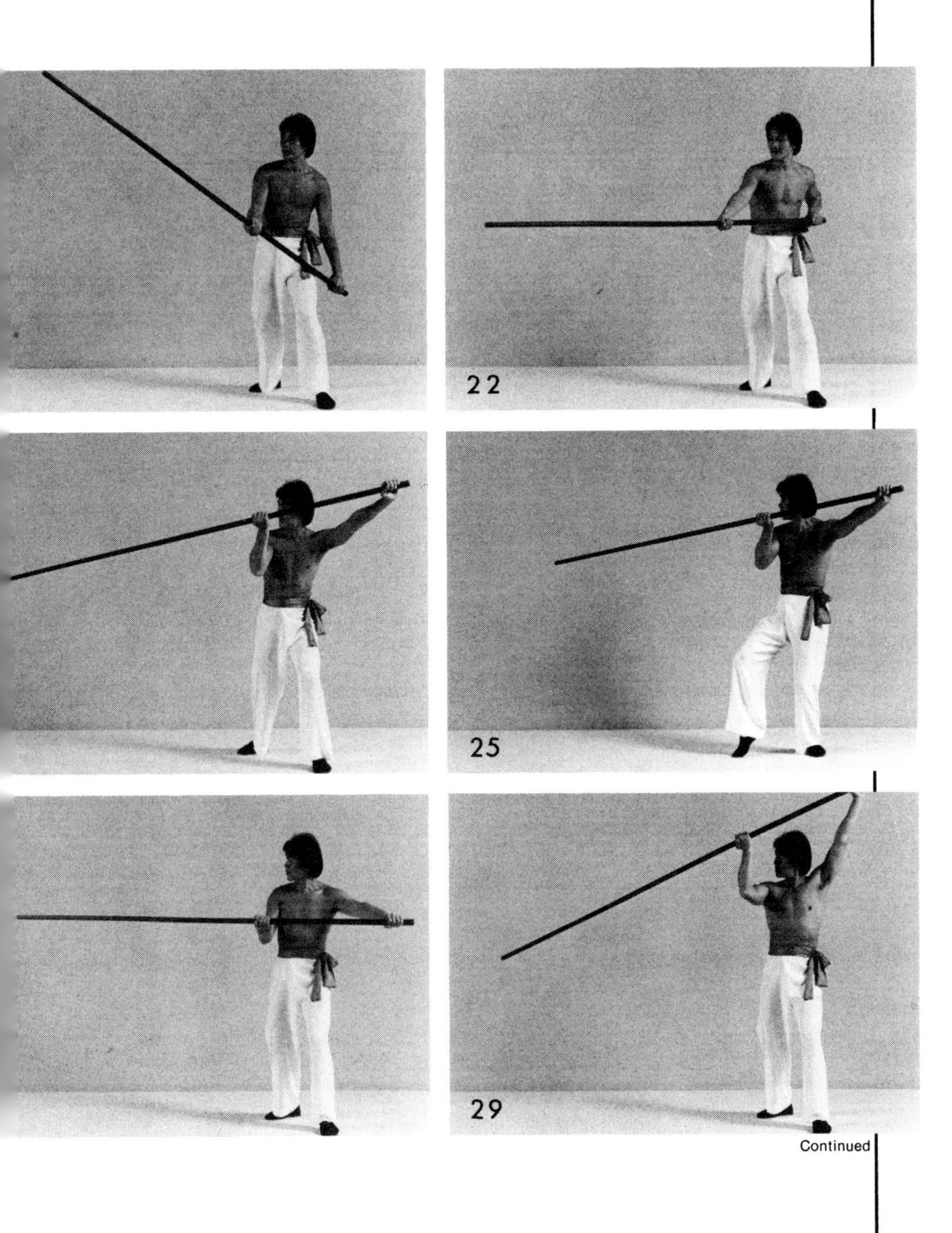

Continued

forward with your right foot and (31&32) execute fok kwun and simultaneously thrust forward. (33) Execute a clockwise rotation of the tip of the pole, simultaneously shifting your weight to your back foot. (34)Execute tarn kwun. (35) Execute fok kwun. (36) Step to your left with your left foot, and strike diagonally downward. (38) Execute a high tarn kwun. (39) Execute fok kwun. (40)

30

33

36

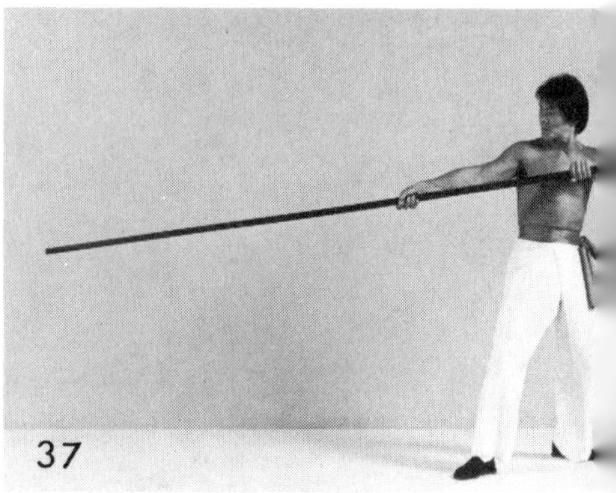

37

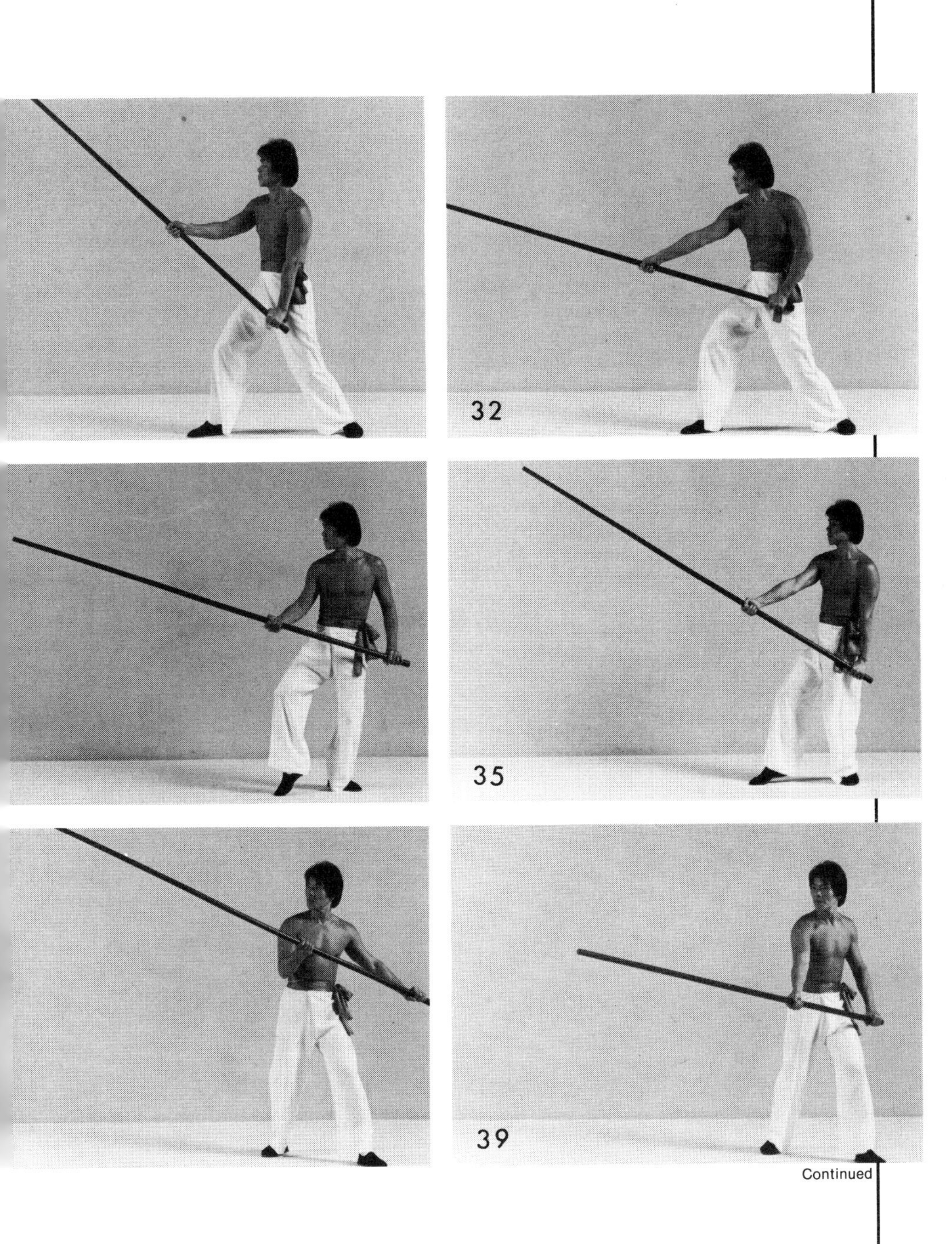

Continued

Step to the left, and pull the pole to the extreme left. (41) Execute til kwun as you simultaneously step across with your right foot. (42) Step forward with your right foot and execute fok kwun. (43) Raise the pole to shoulder level, and (44) thrust horizontally. (45) Step across to the left with your right foot and pull the pole to the extreme left. (46&47) Thrust diagonally downward. (48&49) Bring the pole to your left side in an upright position, and come back to your original starting position.

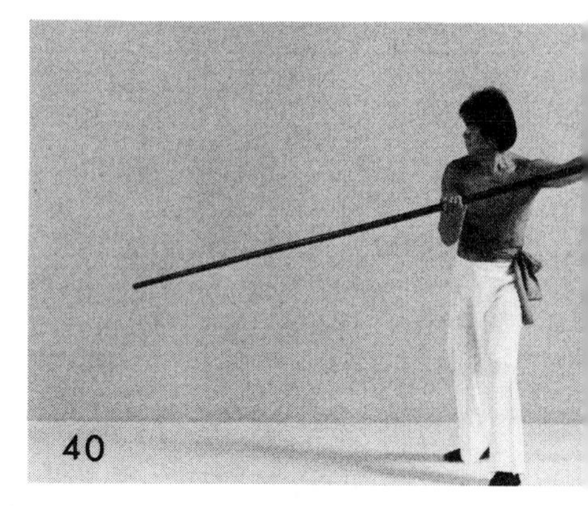
40

43

46

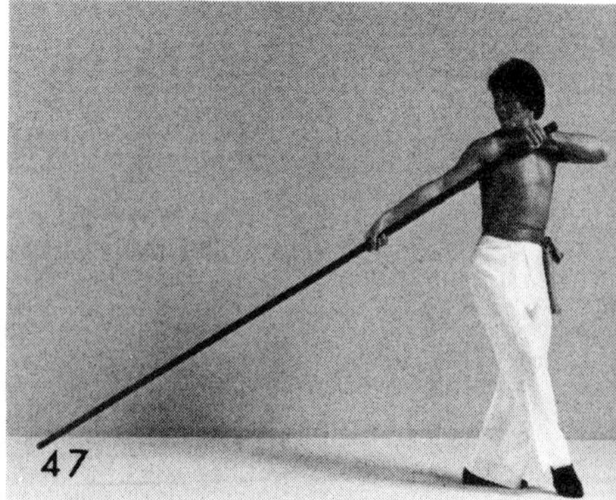
47

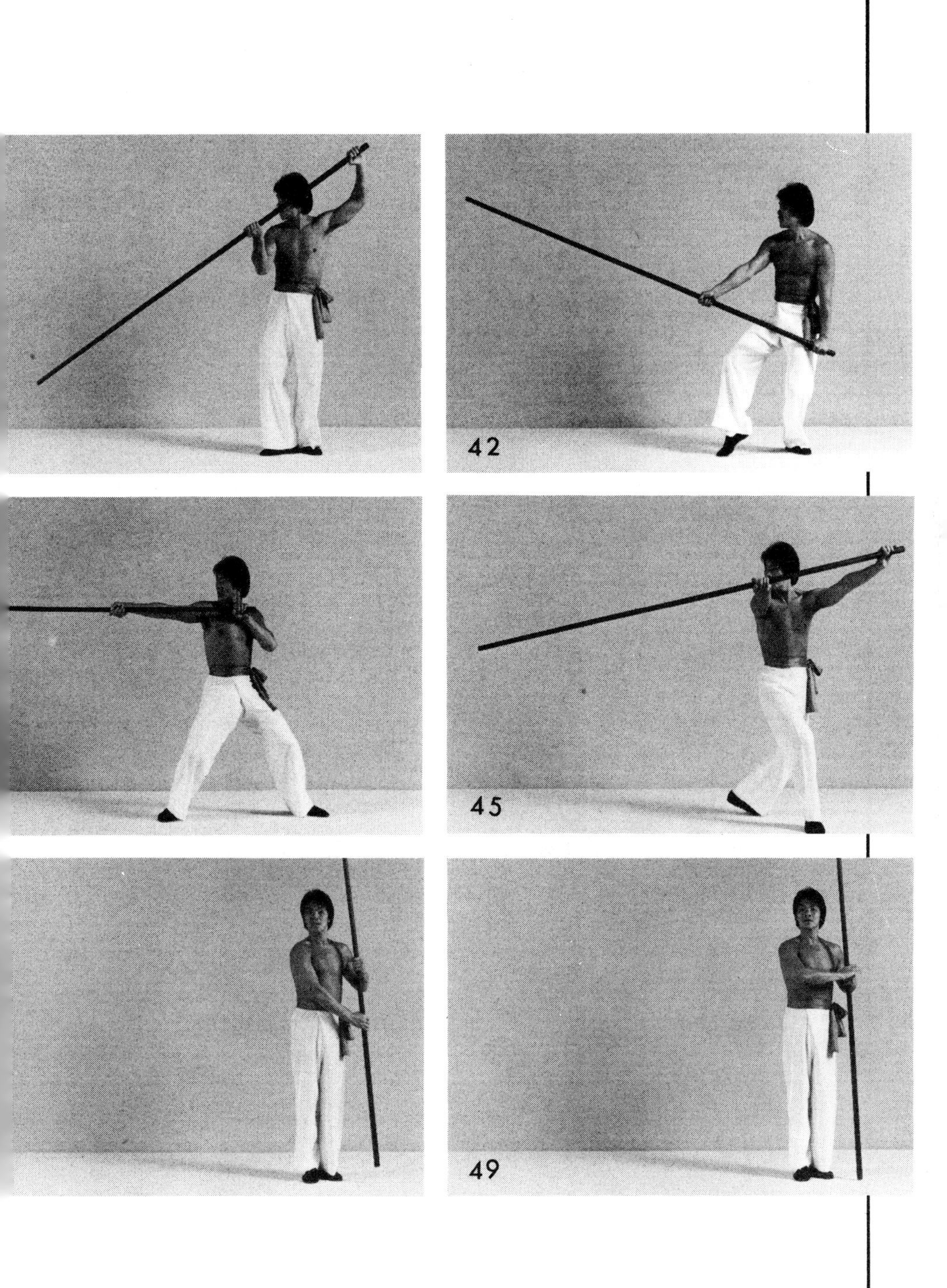
42
45
49

CHAPTER 5

Dragon Pole Against Shorter Weapons

Because dragon pole techniques use only one end of the pole, they achieve the maximum advantage in reach, making it difficult for shorter weapons, such as the staff or hand broadsword, to compete. The only chance an opponent who is armed with a shorter weapon has is to get inside the range of the dragon pole.

Here are examples of dragon pole techniques used against shorter weapons. Much of the skill involved in using the dragon pole against shorter weapons is in maintaining an effective distance, in striking before that distance can be bridged by the opponent, or in recovering that distance by stepping back quickly.

Against a Staff

(1) From the starting position, the opponent with the staff immediately looks for a way of getting inside. (2) The defender uses his dragon pole to keep the opponent outside by thrusting directly toward his throat. The opponent knocks the dragon pole aside forcefully in preparation for stepping in. (3) The defender however, uses the force of the strong parry to rotate his dragon pole quickly downward to strike the opponent's knee, stopping him in his tracks.

Against a Saber—Double Strike

(1) From the starting position, the opponent with the saber also looks to step inside. (2) The defender halts him first with a thrust to the throat which the opponent is forced to parry as he again prepares to step in. (3) The defender goes along with the force of the parry, using that momentum to rotate his pole quickly downward to strike the opponent's knee just as he is about to step inside.

Against a Saber—Triple Strike

Keep the opponent in a defensive mode. (1) From the starting position the defender attempts a pre-emptive thrust at the opponent's head. The opponent blocks the dragon pole. (2) The defender goes along with the momentum of the block by swinging the dragon pole down to strike the knee. The opponent is quick enough to parry that blow as well, but just as he is about to step in, the defender (3) again uses the force of the parry to swing the dragon pole down to strike the opponent's ankle.

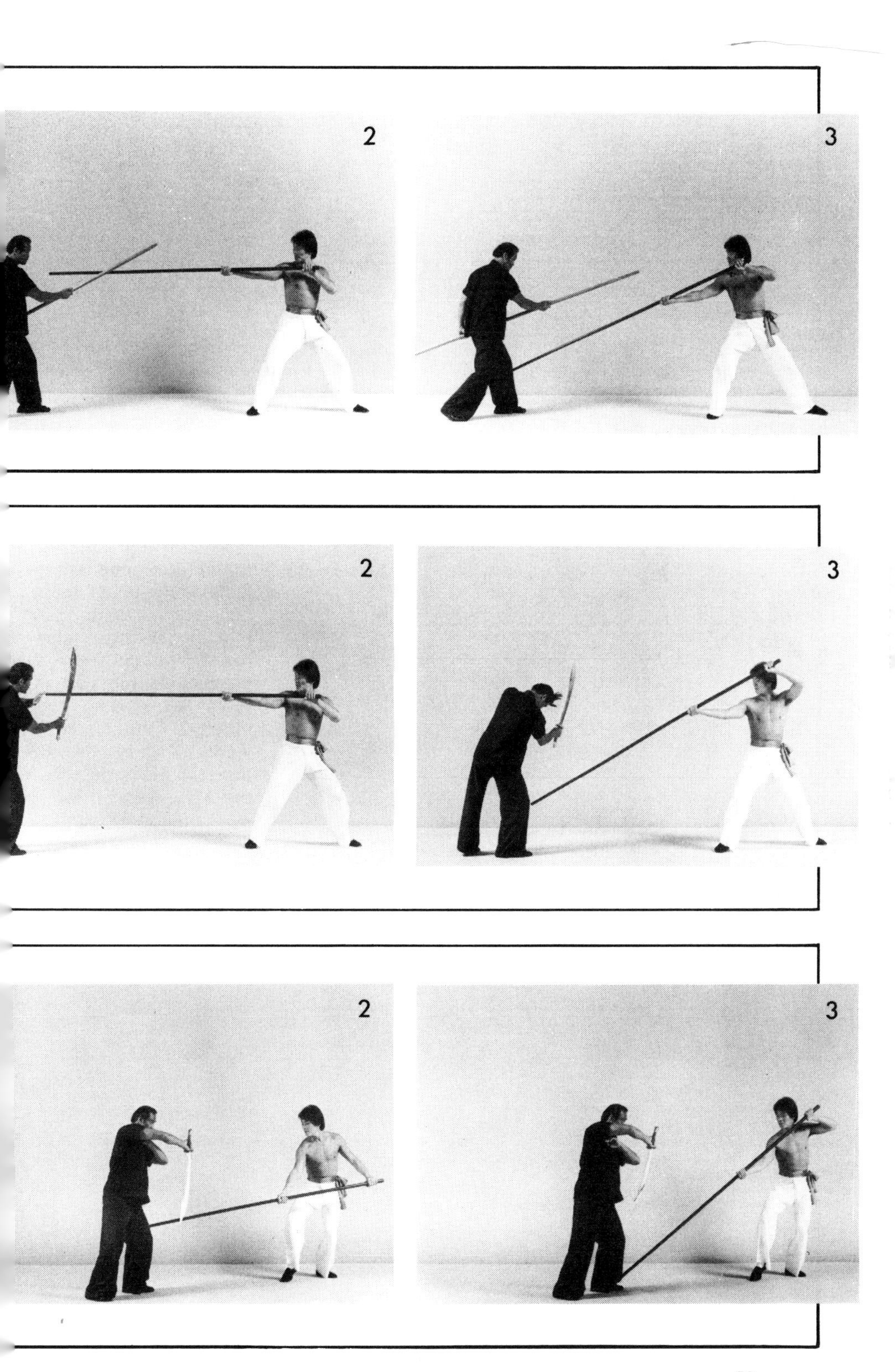
2
3
2
3
2
3

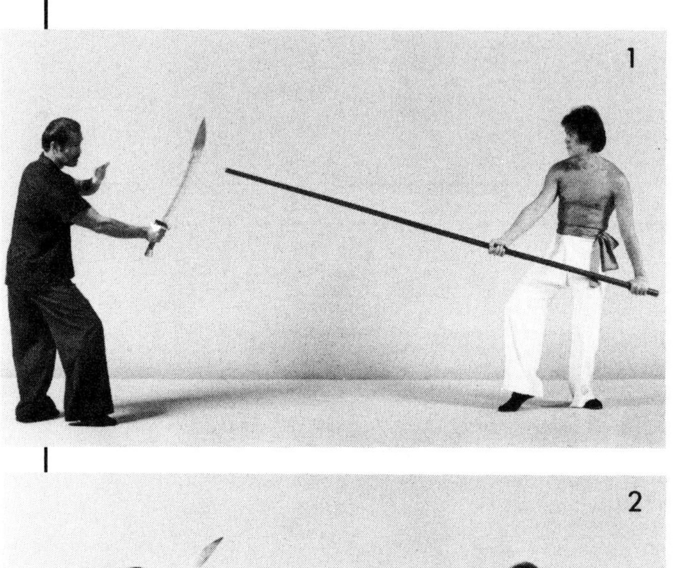
1

2

Against Technique Inside the Range of the Dragon Pole

Should the opponent be fast enough to get inside, the proficient dragon pole practitioner can easily evade the situation by using clever footwork. (1) From the starting position, (2) the defender leads with a pre-emptive thrust to the throat which the opponent parries as he leans forward, and (3) steps in. Momentarily, he has bridged the reach ad-

3

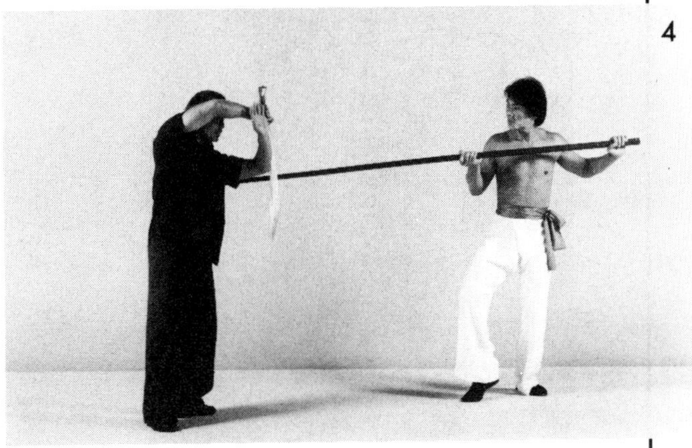
4

vantage of the dragon pole. But the defender pushes him off with tarn kwun, then (4) quickly steps away from the opponent, recovering most of his reach advantage. Pulling back the dragon pole once again puts the opponent at the end of the weapon, and the defender immediately (5) strikes to the opponent's knee to stop his advance.

5

CHAPTER 6

Chi Kwun (Sticky Poles)

Chi kwun is a unique exercise in the wing chun system to train contact reflexes. Contact reflexes are very common in daily activities. For example, when you meet somebody and shake hands with them, you can feel the person's demeanor; when driving a car you can feel from the wheel the condition of the road; when fishing, from the line you can feel the current of the water as well as when the fish attacks the bait. In weapon fighting the outcome of the fight is usually decided a split second after contact of the weapons. Therefore the conditional response, or reflexes, at the point of contact is very important.

The chi kwun exercises given here represent only a small number of chi kwun exercises in the wing chun system. The practitioner of the dragon pole should develop further chi kwun exercises so that he is familiar with different situations.

The benefit of the chi kwun does not rest at gaining contact reflexes, but includes improvement in co-ordination, visual reflexes, mobility, as well as timing and accuracy.

Low Tarn Kwun and Bon Kwun

(1) From the starting position with pole tips crossed and touching, and with both poles aimed at head level, (2) your partner thrusts. You execute a low tarn kwun to counter, then you (3) attempt to strike your partner's hand by sliding along his pole.

(4) Your partner responds with a low tarn kwun to neutralize your attack. (5) Your partner comes back with an overhead strike and you use bon kwun to stop his technique. (6) Then both of you come back to the starting position.

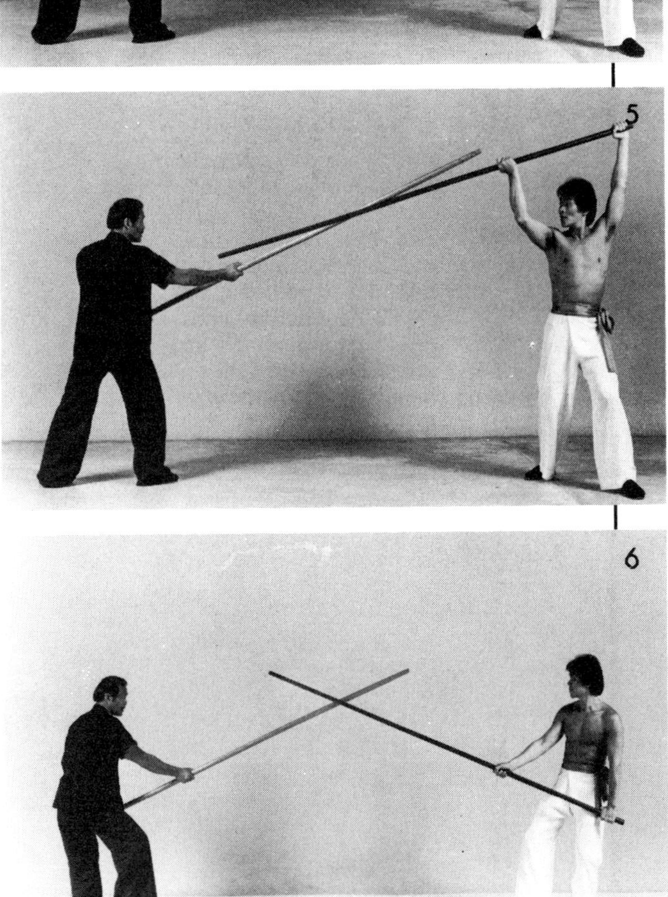

High Tarn Kwun and Bon Kwun

(1) From a starting position with pole tips crossed and touching, and both poles aimed at head level, your partner (2) thrusts. You use high tarn kwun to block. (3&4) You attempt to strike your partner's hand by sliding along his pole (5) Your partner uses low tarn kwun to neutralize the attack. (6) Your partner attempts an overhead strike, and you block with bon kwun. (7) Both of you come back to the starting position.

2
4
5
7

High Tarn Kwun and Jut Kwun

(1) From the starting position, (2) your partner thrusts. You counter using a high tarn kwun. (3&4) You follow up with jut kwun to destroy your partner's defense, and then (5) attempt to attack your partner's wrist. (6&7) Your partner uses tarn kwun to neutralize your attack. Then, (8) both of you come back to the starting position.

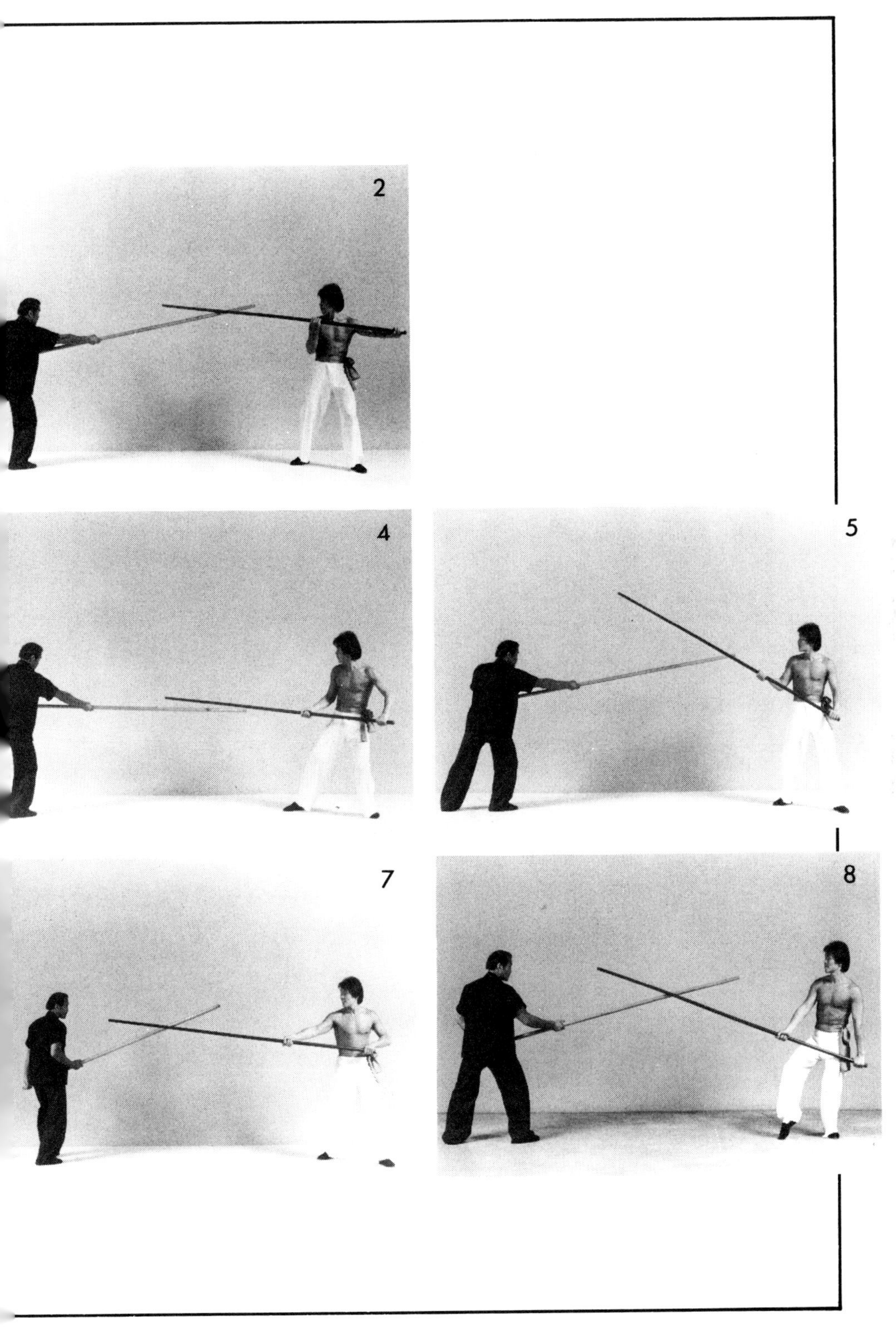
2
4
5
7
8

CHAPTER 7

Techniques and Applications

The dragon pole has the advantage of reach compared to other weapons, so it is essential that the practitioner captialize on this advantage. A description of some of the more common striking methods used in dragon pole combat reveal this strategy. In this chapter you will see many of these techniques used. Although the techniques are described in detail, for the sake of clarity they are not named as the Chinese have named them—that is metaphorically. However, these names do convey a certain cultural flavor and style which are also important. So the combination striking methods are listed:

- *Dragon Darting Thrust* is a series of three or four thrusts to different areas of the opponent's body.
- *Spitting Thrust* is a quick, sudden thrust used in surprise attacks.
- *Entwining Thrust* is used to attack the opponent's head.
- *Star Plucking Thrust* involves blocking the opponent's weapon or striking the opponent and then suddenly withdrawing the pole to attack the opponent's hand when both weapons contact.
- *Yin Yang Thrust* is a simultaneous attack and defense.
- *Rower's Thrust* is used for both attack and defense as well but the pole is used in a continuous circular movement.
- *Flower Planting Thrust* involves meeting the opponent head on, then using the tip of the pole to hit his ankle.
- *Ghost Thrust* is executed by pretending to lose the battle, turning to flee, then suddenly turning back again to thrust at the opponent.

There are many more combination striking methods, but these are the most common.

Parries

Pushing the Opponent's Pole

(1) From the ready position, (2) the defender contacts the opponent's pole. With an unexpected push, the defender (3) moves the opponent's pole out of defending position. (4) He immediately takes advantage by striking quickly to

the opponent's wrist before he has a chance to recover control of the pole. The opponent is quickly disarmed and made vulnerable to a follow-up finishing strike to the body.

3

4

1

2

3

Knocking Opponent's Pole to the Inside

(1) From the ready position, (2) the opponent steps in and (3) attempts a strike to the defender's head. The defender (4&5) uses jut kwun to knock

4

5

the opponent's pole away. (6) The defender then immediately scores a strike by thrusting to the opponent's throat.

6

Knocking Opponent's Pole to the Outside

(1) From the ready position, (2) the opponent steps in with an attempted strike to the defender's head. (3) The defender blocks the strike to the outside with jut kwun, and (4&5) knocks the opponent's pole out of position. (6) With his pole out of position, the opponent cannot defend himself effectively. (7) The defender takes advantage by stepping in with a thrust to the opponent's throat.

5

Guiding Opponent's Pole to the Inside

(1) From the ready position, (2) the opponent moves in with (3) an attempted strike to the defender's head. (4) The defender guides the opponent's pole down from a high position and away

inside to a low position. (5) With his pole so far out of position, the opponent is unable to recover quickly, and the defender takes advantage by (6) striking to the throat.

Guiding Opponent's Pole to the Outside: One

(1) From the ready position, (2) the opponent moves in with (3) an attempted strike to the defender's head. (4) The defender guides the opponent's pole away from a high position to a low po-

sition to the outside. (5) Unable to recover quickly, the opponent is open to a counterattack, and the defender (6) seizes the opportunity by striking to the neck.

Guiding Opponent's Pole to the Outside: Two

(1) From the ready position, (2) the opponent steps across to (3) attempt a backhand thrust to the defender's body. (4) The defender parries and guides the opponent's

3

4

pole away to the outside, then (5) steps in to take advantage of the opponent's vulnerable position, and strikes to the opponent's head.

5

Combinations

Combination Attack—Double Strike to the Ankle

(1) From the ready position, (2) the defender steps across, and (3) attempts a pre-emptive strike to the opponent's lead foot. (4) The oppon-

ent pulls back his foot and avoids the strike. (5) The defender then moves up, catching the opponent flat-footed, and (6) scores a strike to his ankle.

Combination Attack—Two High and One Low

(1) From the ready position, (2) the defender attempts a pre-emptive strike using bil kwun to the opponent's head. The opponent parries it. (3) The defender withdraws his pole, and (4) attacks again to the opponent's

head from the other side. The opponent uses tan kwun to parry. (5) The defender withdraws again. (6) The defender scores by stepping in and thrusting to the opponent's unguarded knee.

1

2

**Combination Attack—
Right and Left**

(1) From the ready position, (2) the defender steps in and attacks from the right side. The opponent parries it. (3&4) The defender swings his pole under the opponent's to the left side, and (5)

strikes the opponent's wrist, causing him to lose his grip on his weapon. The opponent is now unarmed and vulnerable for a finishing strike to his body.

1

Combination Attack—
Bil Kwun and Jut Kwun

(1) From the ready position, (2) the defender steps in and attempts a strike to the opponent's head using bil kwun. (3) The opponent parries the blow. (4&5) The defender swings his pole under to the other side of the opponent's pole, then (6) executes jut kwun to the opponent's pole, pushing it aside and exposing the opponent's body. (7&8) The defender quickly steps in and thrusts to the opponent's throat.

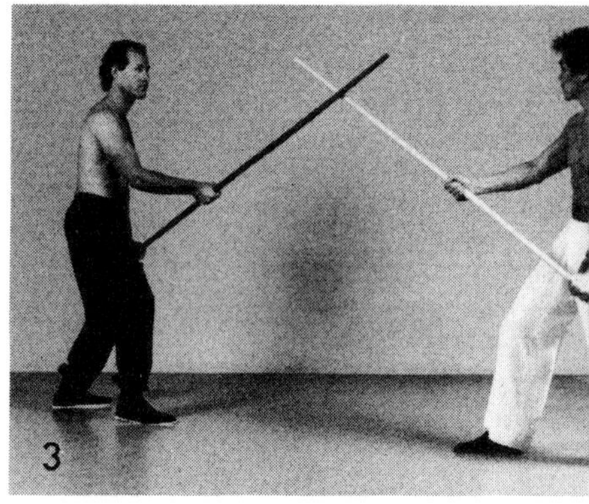

3

6

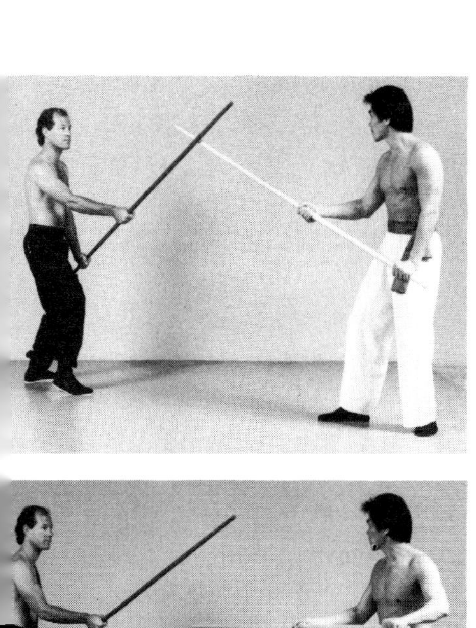

5

8

Combination Attack—High and Low

(1) From the ready position, the defender (2) attempts a pre-emptive thrust to the opponent's head. (3) The opponent successfully parries the strike. (4) The defender

3

then uses the momentum of his opponent's block by continuing to swing his pole downward, coming under the opponent's defense to (5) score a strike to his knee.

4

5

Combination Attack to the Head and Chest

(1) From the ready position, (2) the opponent steps in with an attempted strike to the head of the defender. (3) The defender parries by pushing the opponent's pole aside. (4) The opponent tries to force his pole back into at attack-

ing position. The defender pulls back and prepares for a thrust as he allows the opponent's efforts to re-align both poles into the attack position. (5) The defender thrusts first, and scores to the chest of the opponent.

3

4

5

Combination Attack Switching From Right to Left

(1) From the ready position, (2) the defender attempts a pre-emptive attack from the right side. (3) The opponent parries the strike using jut kwun. (4) The defender switches

to the other side by coming under the opponent's pole. (5) The defender strikes from this side, and (6) scores a strike to the opponent's wrist, causing him to let go of his weapon.

Combination Attack to the Wrist

(1) From the ready position, (2&3) the defender steps in with an attempted pre-emptive strike to the opponent's head. The opponent parries it with tan kwun. (4&5) The defender swings his pole under the opponent's to (6) approach from the other side. (7) The defender strikes to the opponent's wrist, and (8) causes him to let go of his weapon and leaves himself open for a follow-up to the body.

3

6

5

8

Combination Attack Rotation of the Pole

(1) From the ready position, (2) the defender steps in with an attempted pre-emptive strike to the opponent's head. (3) The opponent parries it with jut kwun. (4) The defender rotates the pole to the other side as (5) the opponent keeps in contact. (6) The defender uses the opponent's maintenance of pole contact to rotate both poles (7) beyond the upright position, guiding the opponent's pole away, then (8) comes back quickly to strike to the neck.

2

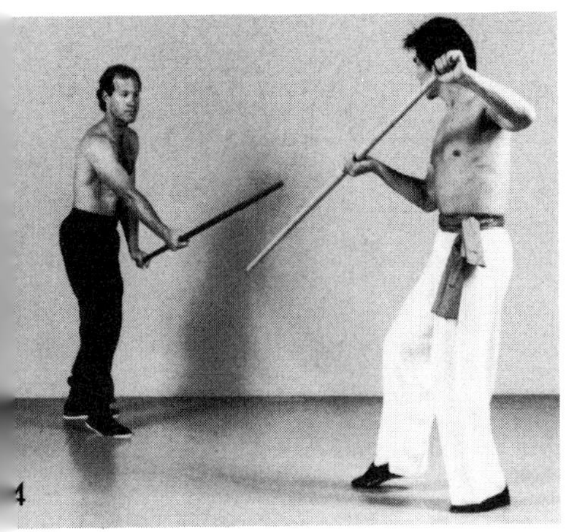

5

8

1

2

3

Combination Attack With Tan Kwun

(1) From the ready position, (2) the defender steps in with an attempted pre-emptive strike to the opponent's head. (3) The opponent parries the strike successfully. (4&5) The op-

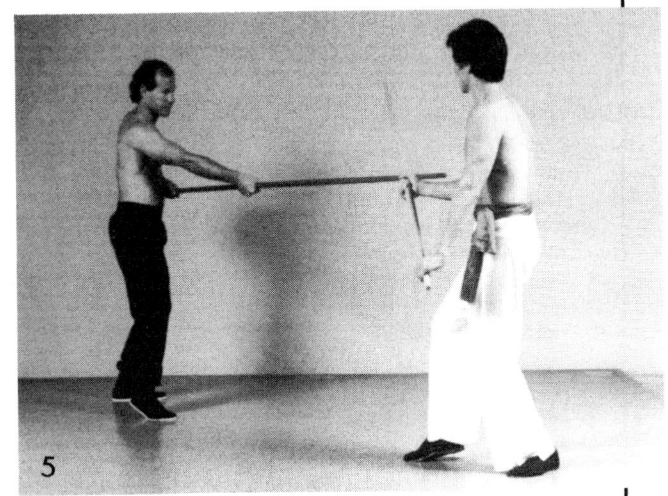

ponent then steps in for a counterattack. The defender uses tan kwun to guide the opponent's pole aside. (6) The defender then steps in and scores a strike to the opponent's elbow.

Counters

Counter Against a Swinging Strike

(1) From the ready position, (2) the opponent moves in with a swinging attack to the defender's midsection. (3) The defender uses bon kwun to block the attack. The defender (4&5) swings his pole over the opponent's pole to (6) strike the opponent's wrist, causing him to let go of his weapon. With the opponent now vulnerable, the defender immediately (7) thrusts a strike to his chest to finish him.

5

Counter Against a Backhand Swinging Strike

(1) From the ready position, (2) the opponent steps across, and (3) attempts a backhand swinging strike to the defender's midsection. (4) The defender uses jut

kwun to parry the blow and knock the opponent's pole out of the way. (5) The defender then immediately executes a forehand swinging strike to the opponent's head.

1

2

Counter Against an Attack to the Leg

(1) From the ready position, (2&3) the opponent moves in with a swinging attack to the defender's legs. The defender uses bon kwun to parry the blow. (4) Before the op-

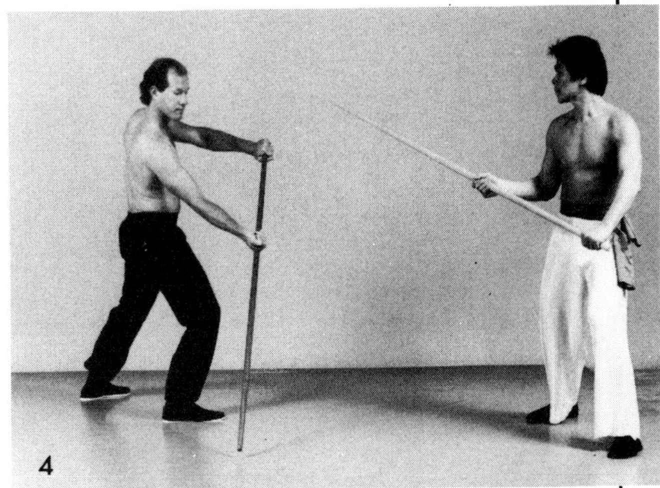

ponent can recover control of his weapon and while he maintains it in a low position, the defender swings his pole up and over to (5) strike the top of the opponent's head.

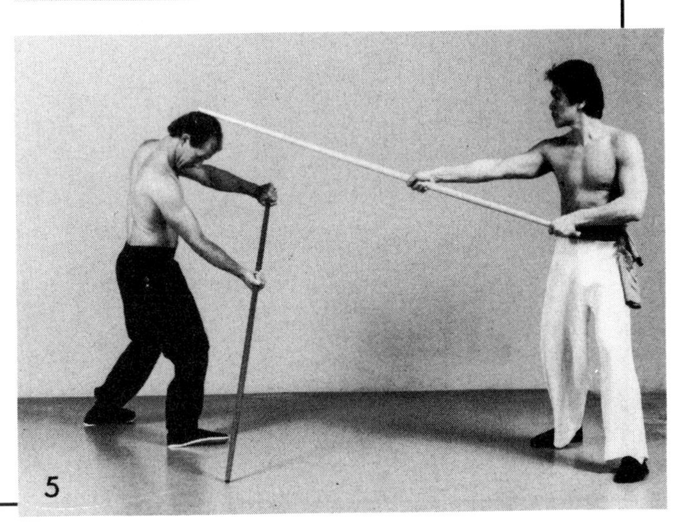

1

2

Counter Against a Backhand Strike to the Leg

(1) From the ready position, (2&3) the opponent steps across, and attempts a low backhand strike to the defender's legs. The defender uses bon kwun to parry the

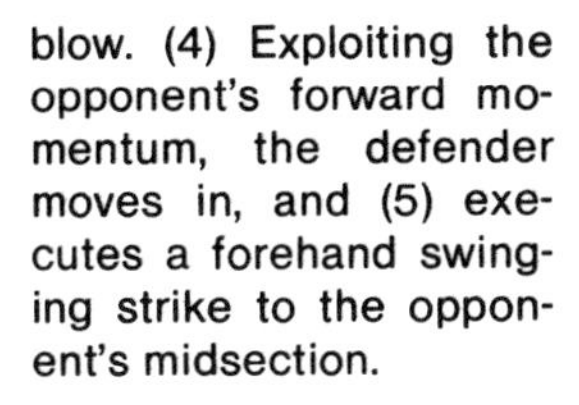
blow. (4) Exploiting the opponent's forward momentum, the defender moves in, and (5) executes a forehand swinging strike to the opponent's midsection.

Counter Against a Strike to the Head

(1) From the ready position, (2&3) the opponent steps in and attempts a thrust to the head of the defender. The defender parries the strike using tan kwun. (4) The defender slides his pole down

the opponent's pole to (5) strike his wrist and cause him to let go of his weapon. (6) The defender then follows up with a strike to the opponent's head.

Counter Against a Strike to the Head

(1) From the ready position, (2) the opponent moves in, attempting a strike to the defender's head. The defender uses tan kwun to parry the

strike. The defender then scores by (4) stepping across at the same time, shifting out of the opponent's line of attack, and striking to his knee.

Counter Against an Attack to the Head

(1) From the ready position, (2&3) the opponent steps in with an attack to the defender's head. (4) The defender pulls his pole to the side, shifting

3

4

his body at the same time, and deflects the opponent's attack. (5) The defender then follows up with a strike to the opponent's throat.

5

Counter Against a Strike to the Head

(1) From the ready position, (2) the opponent steps in and attempts to strike the head of the defender. (3) The defender

parries the blow using tan kwun. (4) The defender then uses the opponent's momentum to score a strike to the opponent's head.

Counter Against High and Low Attack

(1) From a ready position, (2) the opponent moves in with an attack to the defender's body. (3) The defender parries with jut kwun. (4&5) The opponent follows with a low attack to the defender's leg. The defender uses garn kwun to block the low strike. (6&7) The defender counters with a strike to the opponent's head.

1

3

6

5

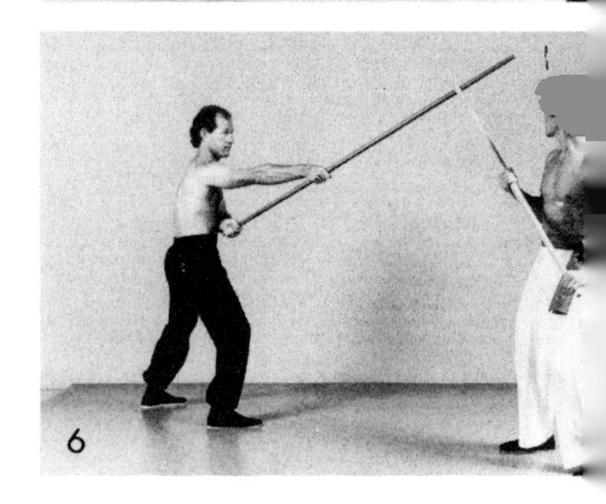

Counter Against Combination Attack to Body and Head

(1) From the ready position, (2) the opponent moves in with an attack to the body of the defender. (3) The defender uses bon kwun to parry the blow. (4) The opponent follows up with an attack to the head. (5&6) The defender uses tan kwun to guide the opponent's pole outside. (7&8) The defender follows with a strike to the opponent's head.

5
8

Combination Counterattack—Two High and One Low

(1) From the ready position, (2&3) the opponent moves in with an attempted strike to the defender's chest. The defender parries the strike

3

with jut kwun. (4&5) The defender then counterattacks to the opponent's head, and the opponent parries, deflecting the thrust to the inside. (6)

4

5

Continued

The defender pulls back his pole under the opponent's, and (7) thrusts again to the other side. The opponent (8) parries by deflecting the thrust to the

outside with tan kwun. (9&10) The defender then switches his line of attack, goes low instead, and scores a strike to the opponent's knee.

BLACK BELT™ VIDEO PRESENTS

NUNCHAKU: KARATE WEAPON OF SELF-DEFENSE
By Fumio Demura
Students are taught to use the *nunchaku* in a traditional manner. Topics covered: how to grip, stances, blocking, striking, calisthenics, karate and nunchaku similarities, and whipping, applied attacking, and applied block and counter.
BBMV101-VHS (60 min.)

BRUCE LEE'S FIGHTING METHOD: Basic Training and Self-Defense Techniques
By Ted Wong and Richard Bustillo
Bruce Lee's *jeet kune do*, as explained in *Bruce Lee's Fighting Method*. This covers the first two volumes, with topics including warm-ups, basic exercises, on-guard position, footwork, power/speed training and self-defense.
BBMV102-VHS (55 min.)

TAI CHI CHUAN
By Marshall Ho'o
World expert in *tai chi chuan* teaches this Chinese practice, which promotes mind-body awareness and rejuvenation. Topics covered: the nine temple exercises, the short form, push hands and self-defense applications.
BBMV103-VHS (90 min.)

KARATE (SHITO-RYU)
By Fumio Demura
This program includes: warm-up exercises; an analysis of basics, including striking points, target areas, standing positions, and hand, elbow, kicking and blocking techniques; three ten-minute workouts; and a demo of basic sparring and self-defense.
BBMV104-VHS (90 min.)

Rainbow Publications Inc.

Black Belt Magazine Video, P.O. Box 918, Santa Clarita, California 91380-9018
Or Call Toll-Free at 1(800)423-2874